MISSPENT YOUTH

by David Mazzotta

Mazzotta, David. Misspent Youth . Kindle Edition.

PART 1

An Undiscovered Country

August 25

Billy wanted to color. Little Missy got to color, so why couldn't he? He grabbed a crayon to help Missy out as she imbued the angelfish in the aquarium with bright but inaccurate colors.

"So you prefer the Audi, eh Billy?" asked Flip.

"A bit more in step with the times, don't you think?" Billy replied without looking up from the purple barracuda he was working on, although he suspected an aquarium with a barracuda must have been the result of a bored and somewhat disturbed coloring book designer.

Marlene gently took the crayon out of Billy's hand and less gently kicked him under the table.

Billy gathered himself. "I mean, Mercedes quality has gone south. And too many douchebags are driving BMWs."

"Mommy, what's a douchebag?" asked Missy.

"Nothing honey, Billy is just acting up." Another kick.

"You can't beat 'em for resale value, though," Flip replied.

Flip was on his best behavior. His wife Pammy, on his left, had made it clear that he should be on his best behavior because she never got to go out with adults anymore what with watching their three monstrous children, and since there was a new babysitter in town who had not yet experienced the horror of their offspring this may very well be the last night she would ever get out until the damn kids were in college. As such, Flip was being careful to watch his language and not verbalize any of the smart-assed remarks that had been relentlessly bombarding his brain ever since puberty.

Billy was coming out, so to speak. Marlene and Billy had been sleeping together for a while now and Marlene decided it was time for Billy to meet her friends. Billy didn't really think twice about it. Although he sensed a cursory masculine bond with Flip, new friendships were rare in men circling the age of forty. Marlene actually felt it was time for much more than meeting her friends but she also knew the delicacy of bringing up any sort of commitment with a 40-year old bachelor. She was taking baby steps.

Pammy knew this too, and the real point of this dinner was to lay a base of common knowledge about Billy for future girl talk.

The waiter arrived. "Would anyone like a beverage to start?"

"Martini—dirty."

"Apple-tini."

"Melon-tini."

"Sam Adams."

"Chocolate milk!" cried Missy. Missy, Marlene's

daughter from her late marriage, was along because her babysitter was unavailable, thus undermining the adults night out.

Marlene belied the order with tolerant authority. "No, honey, you can't have chocolate milk. Do you have cranberry juice?"

"Coming right up," replied the waiter as he scurried off.

The innocuous conversation resumed. "You still live in the city, don't you Billy?" Flip asked and was rewarded with kick from Pammy. He had no idea why, nor did he give it any thought. He had long ago accepted that he was not put on this Earth to understand why.

Pammy altered the conversation's trajectory. "You should think about buying a house. I wish I had bought a place, even a dump, right out of college instead of throwing my money away on rent."

Billy briefly marveled at how complex the situation had become, even before the drinks had arrived. Flip was asking innocent questions and was getting Pammy upset because she knew Marlene would believe she had instructed Flip to try to get information about Billy's ability to commit, when in fact she had done no such thing. So Pammy was attempting to change the subject except she happened on to a subject of high sensitivity to Billy who, despite outward appearances, was quite aware of his weak credentials as a grown-up.

"They just started pre-selling the new development out near us. There's a good profit to be made by getting in early," Pammy elaborated, casting furtive glances at Marlene in a fruitless search for any indication of impropriety. She soldiered on, "I love our neighborhood. Very good schools. The kids can play."

Billy nodded in non-committal agreement.

"It's funny," Flip declared. "When you drive to work in the morning, if you leave at the same time you see the exact same people in the cars in front of you, and behind too. Like clockwork. You end up caravanning into town with the same people every day. That's fair warning not to pick your nose on the way to work. It'll be all over the neighborhood by the end of the day."

Pammy looked askew at Flip.

"Mommy look!" cried Missy. Her finger was in her nose and she was giggling.

"Melissa, you stop that now!"

Billy stuck out his tongue at Missy and grinned.

"Mommy, Billy stuck his tongue out at me!"

"Don't encourage her, Billy."

"You live right down on Main Street, don't you Billy?"

"Yep. I know it's summer when I can smell the food from the sidewalk cafes," Billy intentionally romanticized. Living in a trendy, stylish loft in a trendy, stylish downtown neighborhood above a trendy, stylish coffee house was the sort of thing that made the local young professional set drool with envy. How much cooler was it to get your produce at the open-air farmers market than at some giant hyper-efficient supermarket? How utterly gratifying was it to order take-out from a genuine deli on the corner rather than some sterile, corporate fast food joint? How fashionably inconvenient was it to have to rent a parking space three blocks away instead of having one of those tawdry attached garages? Of course that smell from the sidewalk cafes also attracted six-legged crawlies, the deli was criminally overpriced, and his car stereo required a removable faceplate for security—but it all had such character.

Flip gave Billy a look of conspiratorial envy.

Marlene gave Billy a look of suspicious evaluation.

Pammy gave Flip a look of reprobation.

Missy said, "You can't marry your own brother, can you Mommy?"

"No, honey, now please don't inter—"

"You can't marry your cousin, either," Missy further suggested.

"Honey—"

"Only in West Virginia," Flip offered.

"And then only if you have more teeth than her," Billy enjoined.

"And you can't marry your dog," Missy concluded.

"But you can marry a man and treat him like a dog. That's valid," Flip asserted.

"Could you take him for walks?" Missy asked sincerely.

"Yes, but you have to clean up when he goes poo."

"Ewww! "

"OK, stop it. Just stop it," Marlene said shaking her head.

They all laughed, then Missy knocked over her cranberry juice. Everyone jumped out of the way of the spreading liquid. Missy started to cry. Billy picked up a straw and started sipping the juice directly from off the table before it dripped on him. Missy giggled in delight.

••••

Missy was in a deep sleep on the way home, strapped snugly into her car seat.

"Have you thought about it yet?"

"About what?"

"Don't be difficult," Marlene instructed, habitually

using the same tone she used to correct Missy. "I'm talking about moving in."

"Yeah...well, no, not yet...well...I'm still worried about..."

"Missy will love having you around."

"Don't be difficult," Billy replied playfully. "You know what I mean."

"I'm sure there're plenty of other children at her school in the same situation or worse. For all we know, her teacher might be making ends meet as a stripper."

"Hmm, I'd like to meet her teacher."

"Would you now?"

"Look, if we aren't married and we're openly sharing a bed, how are you ever going to tell her not to have casual sex with a straight face? By that I mean you telling her with a straight face, not her having sex with a straight face."

"This is casual sex to you?"

Well fuck me. Billy thought. "No. But how old will Missy be before she can make that distinction? When she's fifteen and thinks she's in love with the dorky looking kid with saggy pants and a peach-fuzz mustache, how are you going to tell her to wait? It's casual sex to you, it's true love to her."

"I'll just say, 'Missy, when you are thirty-eight years old and been through marriage, childbirth, motherhood, and divorce, you have my blessing to sleep with anyone you want. Until then the legs stay crossed.'"

"I'm sure that'll work well with a hormonally engorged teenager. Look, there are reasons you tell kids to wait until marriage—"

"Oh, please. How silly and stupid would that sound? Did you? Did I? Does anyone?"

"Doesn't matter. You've got to play the game. If you tell her it's OK to have sex in the correct circumstances—mind you it took you thirty-eight years to discover the right circumstances..." *Take that*, he thought. "...she's going to find the correct circumstances everywhere she goes. You tell her don't sleep with anyone until you are married, she at least shows some reticence. She may even wait all the way until college."

"When did you get so smart, Mister Carefree

Bachelor?"

Despite—or perhaps because of—the familiarity of such comments, Billy always felt slightly wounded by the implication of immaturity. It wasn't like he was opposed to living together. He had lived with a woman before, in his twenties, and while the results couldn't be called a success, it wasn't so bad as to put him off it. Actually, he was more surprised Marlene wasn't keen on marriage. Perhaps her life with Missy's father put her off that for good.

He didn't consider himself particularly conservative, yet the idea of living together seemed...would 'intemperate' be a good word? Yeah, if he was in a Henry James novel.

Maybe 'childish' was the right word. Two adults who'd known each other for years, moving inexorably closer to middle age—yet they found barriers to complete commitment. Were they still playing the 'I'm not sure' game? As if they may suddenly betray themselves as something other than a beautiful princess and a knight in shining armor. Marlene had previously proved herself capable of taking the big step and harbored the reasonable fear of a similar result. But what was his excuse? Did he believe there was some sort of greater fulfillment waiting elsewhere?

After a few minutes of silence, they arrived at her house. As Billy lifted Missy out of the seat she asked, "Billy, what's hormonally engorged?"

"That's a disease teenagers get, honey."

Once Missy was tucked in bed, Billy and Marlene embraced. Billy was anxious to leave; conversations like the one they had in the car always made him anxious to leave, but he was determined not to betray the feeling with words or body language.

"You want to leave, don't you?" Marlene observed.

Billy doubted it would do any good to say no. He was certain it would do no good to say yes.

He replied, "Look, I'm tired. And this conversation needs more attention than I can give it now." He could see he needed to go further. "Let's find a time when we can get together, no friends, no Missy. When can you get an overnight babysitter next?"

"Weekend after next. Maybe. I'll ask Jenna."

"Let's get away. I'll get us a room at the Charles-Lansing. We can have dinner, go for a swim, and talk all night. OK?"

Marlene shrugged.

....

Billy was relieved to be gone, for which he felt appropriately guilty. Back home, he quickly paged through his caller ID, grabbed a Diet Coke out of the fridge, kicked his shoes off, sat in silence while the DVR offered him the latest pointless crap, undressed, brushed and flossed his teeth, crawled into an unmade bed, and thought about picking up his new Audi.

August 27

"Okay, guys, I left the window to Missy's room open so let's keep it clean."

Marlene slipped in the hot tub opposite Pammy. To her right was Sarah, the Yoga instructor—lithe, serenely flexible, and a bit reserved. Her eyes were closed, her mind was clear. On her left sat Dora, filling champagne glasses for everyone and wondering if her arms were too flabby and her fingers too pudgy. "Here's to Naked Tuesday," she toasted.

"Actually, Naked Every Other Tuesday."

"Actually, Naked Every Other Tuesday during the summer..."

"...except when we have the kids at Disney..."

"...or my allergies are acting up..."

"...or I have a date..."

"As if!"

"OK, OK. Here's to three or four Naked Tuesday's a year!"

Glasses clinked.

"This is the closest I get to sex," Pammy declared and reached for a box of Godiva chocolates, which promptly became the focal point of fervent activity.

"Oh no," cried Dora, three chocolates later. "How many calories are in these?"

"Honey, nothing you eat when you're naked counts,"

Marlene offered with a full mouth.

"It's stress, you know. I eat fine. I have no problem keeping strictly to Weight Watchers. But I can't shed a pound."

Dora was the Divorced One. She wasn't the only divorced one, Marlene was divorced too, but Dora wore her divorce like a yoke.

Dora and Dick had divorced two years prior. Whenever their divorce was discussed, it was always in the passive voice; never Dora divorced Dick or the reverse, they simply *were* divorced. Dora filed, but no one felt it was her fault. No one could really blame Dick either—he never did anything particularly bad, he had done his level best. After nineteen years of marriage, Dora simply decided she was not the same person anymore; she needed something else, something she never had.

One evening Dora was doing laundry. She had been watching *Dancing with the Stars* on TV when Jenna came in and made fun of the show and fun of her for watching it. She changed the channel from meek instinct and made some comment like "not paying attention, really," then went to the laundry room. While separating whites she held up a pair of

Dick's briefs. They had been bright and pristine and taut when first pulled from their plastic wrapping. Now the sullen contours of the cotton evidenced the stresses and depressions they had endured on the way to their ultimate submission. They had served honorably, they deserved better.

Dora suddenly realized that she had never lived alone in her life. This notion came to take on the character of a lost rite of passage, an experience she would be incomplete without. She wanted to come home in the evening and read, or watch TV—any TV show that caught her fancy, without explanation. She wanted her home to be clean and orderly. She wanted the phone not to ring. She wanted —for once!—to be able to play her favorite show tunes without snarky commentary. In her wildest moments, she wanted to go out on a date and to be able to invite the gentleman up for coffee. She had never had any of that and she should have. She deserved it.

What she had was Dick, who she married because... well, she wasn't sure. She supposed she loved him, even now. She loved him for practical purposes back then, he was solid after all, and he paid attention to her, and you could always count on him to be reasonable, and he never watched porn. Whatever the case, she loved him enough to go through with marriage, which was a pretty good day as she recalled it. Some women don't even get that, and that counted for something.

When she finally approached Dick about divorce, she knew her only hope to carry it through was to adopt a tone of pious inevitability, and that she had damned well better believe it herself. She strained to maintain a granite-firm resignation in her words. She had spent so much time worrying about the delivery she was taken aback when Dick acquiesced. He was quiet as she went through with her planned soliloquy, his body articulated as if his full attention was focused on her as he had always done since they learned about active listening at that marriage retreat eight years ago. When she finished he remained silent, allowing the weight of the matter to settle into his ample jowls. He nodded in understanding as was his habit and said, "I'm hurt and I don't know what to say. But I know you are unhappy. If that is what will make you happy, I understand."

Not that she expected him to fuss or fight—she really hadn't thought about his reaction at all, and she also hadn't thought about what to do next. Instinct told her to backtrack to a "trial separation," but she remained firm. There was an extended awkward moment, neither of them having a frame of reference for how to behave at a marriage's end. That night she slept on the couch; it was only fair because she was the one who started it all. The next day they sat down at the kitchen table with Jenna, their defiant seventeen-year-old, to have an open discussion about the situation and assure her that it wasn't her fault and everything would be OK. With barely a moment's consideration, her only response was, "Fine. Where am I going to live?" It wasn't really fair for Dora to get the house, so she got an apartment. Dick assumed the entire mortgage payment, and Jenna stayed with her father.

Dora was alone for the first time in her life. She threw herself into decorating her new apartment (one bedroom, one bath) exactly as she wanted; a trying task considering her innate middle-class frugality caused her to visit outlet malls in three states to find just the right accoutrements at a reasonable price. She kept the place beyond immaculate. And she read a chapter or two every night before bed. And she played show tunes, but not so loud the neighbors could hear. And although she hadn't had a date, nor any prospects for that matter, she still had the ability of asking one in if she wanted. And she still made the effort to be at home for her favorite TV shows even though the DVR had her covered.

She tried to appreciate her position. She had found the independence she had imagined, but she couldn't seem to break the habit of shopping for her house; they knew her by name in the housewares section at Target. And all those books about ironic single women who buy expensive clothes and have a lot of sex grew increasingly similar. And the DVR filled up with unwatched shows. And every time she saw Jenna she wanted to cry. Hence, Weight Watchers.

"Why do you suppose that is?" she continued, somewhat distressed. She turned to Sarah, the Yoga instructor, in a vain plea for wisdom.

"Well part of it is also your body type," Sarah began in her practiced fitness professional tone. "And part of it is—"

"You should get a Stair Master. Those are great—a half hour every other day, in front of the TV, or you can read while you're doing it," Pammy advised.

"You think so?"

"Actually, I think in your case—" Sarah tried again.

"I do Tae Bo," Marlene offered. "At the gym. You should join the gym with us, don't you think Sarah?"

"Sure, you could—"

"Lots of cute guys."

"You know, Flip actually had a decent ass in college."

"Didn't we all."

"MOMMY!"

Marlene hopped up and dashed off, wrapping a towel around her as she went.

"How does she handle it?" pleaded Dora. "My daughter is practically on her own—I don't even have custody, but I never feel like I can keep up. And she stays so thin."

"She's got Molly Maid," Pammy replied.

"Really?"

"Oh yeah. A couple of times a month makes all the difference. And she's got your daughter, who...

babysits," Pammy continued, taking special care. "And she's got Billy. She doesn't have to worry when Jenna's not around because he's happy to have the kid with them—"

"Shhh—"

"Does anyone know who Tori Tornado is—" Marlene asked as she returned, then realized no one was talking. "What did I miss?"

"We were gossiping about you and Billy."

"Oh. Nothing to gossip about. He still won't move in."

"I miss living alone," declared Pammy. "You know there were only four months in my life where I lived alone. Can you believe that? I hated it, but now I miss it."

"It's not so great," Sarah said. "I mean, it's OK if you can keep yourself occupied but it's just as easy to give up and dwell on how lonely you are."

"Sarah?"

"No, I mean, not me. I have lots to occupy me. Lots of interests. Plus, I'm not afraid to go out on my own. But I know a lot of women who are. They get addicted to reality TV and do nothing but clean house during commercials."

Dora said nothing.

Sarah was an only child who never felt like she fit in. She did, in fact, fit in. And she knew she fit in, but she didn't *feel* like she fit in. She had at least three distinct circles of friends and she was unconditionally welcome in all of them, but that provided no comfort. She could not escape the feeling of being a burden, even though she had no rational basis for that belief.

Her conscious purpose was to harbor no hostility and always be a positive force. There would be no anger, no fear, and no despair in her life. She would always be constructive, and when she wasn't feeling constructive, she would act constructive until she felt it again. Faith in her positive purpose would inform all of her actions. If she fit in, fine; if not, fine. The higher path was what counted, such individual interpersonal concerns would fall into place one way or another. She knew she could only approach this life, never attain it, but the journey was what had meaning. Her violations of this faith were numerous, some small, some large. Like when she dated Billy...was it loneliness? Companionship? Was it her valid, but regrettable, physical attraction? The only real shame was the falsehood. The way she forced little fits of laughter at his cynical remarks or bit her tongue if he contradicted her. That was the compromise that caused her contrition: she quietly dropped her guard for a role in his superficial life. Did Marlene know about it?

She exhaled to quiet her mind. Hostility served no one. Billy was just a random soul crossing her path. Like the bee that stung her yesterday or her breast cancer scare or being in this moment in this hot tub, for that matter.

Why did it always have to be about men?

It wasn't like she didn't have opportunities with men, although most of them were not her type—the awkward men who would come up to speak with her after Yoga class. They would keep asking strained questions about Yoga, not caring about the answers, just rooting around for some indication of interest. She gave them credit, struggling through the uncomfortable postures with their rigid limbs and puffy mid-sections, unaccustomed to stretching and bending, and equally unaccustomed to being still and looking inward. It took a form of courage and a sort of open-mindedness, even if there were ulterior motives.

Billy was one of those guys back then, but he didn't persist with inane questions, after a brief introduction he just asked her out. He just arrogantly assumed she would be attracted to him. He was not a bad person, despite his wandering eye, but what was he thinking with all the expensive restaurants and all the fancy gadgets? Did he think that would impress her? She was a peaceful and principled non-materialist and committedly spiritual. Couldn't he see that?

Damn. Why did it always have to be about men?

"When I lived alone my place was clean and tidy," Pammy said. "You know, that's what I miss. I miss coming home to a clean house. I miss being able to cook a small meal for myself then read or watch TV and not be surrounded by chaos.

Dora smiled, weakly; barely breathing.

"You'll never get that with boys around," Marlene said.

I'll never get that without Molly Maid, Pammy

thought. "Yeah, four of 'em. Ages six, seven, eight and forty-one," Pammy said.

"I don't know if I could handle boys."

"They're not so bad."

"I'd miss having girl talk with Missy," Marlene said.

They all laughed.

"What do you talk about, boys?"

"Sure, sometimes. We talk about clothes and music and dancing and the other girls in her class and what their mothers are like—"

Dora recalled, "You know, I remember when Jenna and I had little talks like that. I remember the first time we talked about boys because there was one little boy who kept chasing her around on the playground. She said he wasn't fast enough to catch her, so she let him."

"Oooh."

"That's so sweet."

Dora continued, "Now she barely says anything to me, and I don't think she's said three meaningful words to her father in the last year. Of course, he never did talk, just *educate*."

"Why does everything have to be about men?" Sarah asked. This was met with universal bafflement.

"I mean everything we talk about has to do with men. Good sex. Bad sex. How much you weigh. Who's not pulling his weight. Who can't behave right. Who can't catch who on the playground. Even you're conversations with your daughters. Everything is about men. Don't we have anything in our lives that isn't about men?"

A momentary silence ensued.

"I saw a good movie the other day."

"Really, what?"

"It was on cable. *Ocean's Thirteen*. Very cute. Very exciting."

"Mmmm. Brad Pitt."

"What do you suppose is up with him and Angelina."

As the evening wore on the conversation waned. Marlene began to wonder when people would leave. Sarah wanted to leave but didn't want to be the first to go because she knew it would cement her position as the odd one out. Dora was thinking about a TV special she saw on the Kennedys and how sad it was to have so much tragedy in a family. Pammy was thinking about getting oral sex from Brad Pitt, but realizing she couldn't see his face in that position it didn't much matter who she was getting oral sex from.

Finally Marlene had to say, "Oh, look how late it's gotten," and everyone cleared out slowly, thinking that it was just like Marlene to want to end things so quickly.

August 28

Billy sat quietly for forty-five minutes. It was not clear to him why the only person who was capable of handing him the keys to his new Audi was the same man who sold it to him. A suggestion that perhaps another employee could help was met with either a pleasant "It shouldn't be much longer" or a more terse "I'm sorry that's our policy." He also couldn't understand why, when he had arranged to meet with his salesman at 3 pm and had left work early to do so, his salesman hadn't avoided engaging the new customer that still occupied his attention forty-five minutes past Billy's arrival.

Billy realized that since they already had his money he had little recourse; the potential money from the other customer was more important. He made a silent vow to buy his next car over the internet and built up a mental list of ferocious insults to let loose on his salesman once he appeared. Meanwhile, he passed the time by eavesdropping on the conversation of two women on the other side of the waiting room who sounded like they were in a similar predicament.

"...nearly half an hour. Can you imagine that? What kind of service is that?" Woman A said loud enough to be heard by the receptionist and several other salesmen. None registered the slightest reaction.

"Oh, it's terrible," concurred Woman B. "Same thing happened to me last time. Last time I didn't get any service until my daughter started having a screaming tantrum."

Woman A raised her volume a notch so that even potential customers could hear. "Maybe a screaming tantrum is what you need to get any service." Then in a normal tone asked, "How old is your daughter?"

"Seven. Going on seventeen."

"I know what you mean. Eight and twelve myself."

"So have you found a Tori Tornado doll yet?"

"Nope. I still don't understand what is so special about her." Woman A shook her head in confusion. "My husband is in Europe and he can't find one there either."

"Flavor of the Month, I suppose. Although my daughter keeps talking about something called a 'swarm,' whatever that is. I read people are trying to smuggle them out of Korea," observed Woman B with a short burst of forced laughter.

"So I tried to tell her that you can't find Tori Tornado anywhere, and my sweet, little, innocent seven-year-old says to me, 'Did you try Craigslist?'"

A lanky teenager in overalls appeared and motioned for Billy to follow him. They walked to the front of the dealership and the kid handed Billy the keys to a shiny silver Audi.

"Thanks, Jimbo," said Billy. Billy had to shelve his stored supply of insults since he was friends with

Jimbo, who had obviously pulled some strings to save Billy from having to wait for his slack-jawed, snot-gobbling, goat-blowing salesman.

"No problem. Sweet, eh?"

"Yes it is."

Jimbo circled the Audi, ceremoniously swatting off spots of dust with a clean white rag. Billy smiled at the obviously symbolic action—a policy designed to impress the buyer. And it worked; Billy was impressed that someone had put so much thought into the policy.

Jimbo was on the gangly side, a bit taller than average; the type that never does seem to completely fill out his clothes. He lacked the awkwardness of most youths in casual conversation with adults, but his posture was true teenager, carrying the weight of the adult world on his shoulders. He hadn't quite mastered the art of shaving so his anemic, adolescent dirty blonde goatee had something of a patchy appearance. Billy assumed most girls saw him as James Dean-ish, which meant he was probably not in need of female attention, which only served to further emphasize his desirability to them. For the millionth time, Billy felt a clichéd desire to be that age again, knowing what he knew now.

Billy liked Jimbo.   He was initially introduced to Billy as Marlene's babysitter's boyfriend when they happened to cross paths at the mall a while back.   Billy promptly forgot about him until he encountered him at the Audi dealer.   He became Billy's inside source; the guy Billy could count on to find out when he could bring his car in for the quickest service, when the price breaks were coming, and generally how to cut through any sleazy policies. He was only Head Porter but like the doorman at a fine hotel he was the guy who could make things happen.   It had taken them a couple of minutes to bridge the innate communications gap between seventeen and forty, but they found a lot of common ground.   They talked about cool cars and video games.   They talked about music—Billy was the only grown-up Jimbo knew who realized that the music he listened to in college wasn't the pinnacle of Western culture.   They talked about graphic novels, which Billy didn't know much about, but at least he didn't call them comic books.

"I bet you're not looking forward to getting back to school," asked Billy, wisely employing the anti-adult formulation of that question.

"Not really. Well, it won't be that bad. Senior year means it's almost over. Everyone says I should be enjoying it all, making the most of everything."

"Dude, it's high school. Survive and move on," Billy said with a knowing grin. They shared a silent acknowledgement of the stupidity of adults.

"All set," said Jimbo. "Damn, I wish it was mine."

"Well, you'll just have to take it out for a spin sometime."

"Really?"

"Sure. Maybe we can—"

"Jim! Are you talking or working?" bellowed a fat lout with a ludicrous pornstar moustache, his tie flopping over the left shoulder of his short-sleeved polyester shirt.

Billy looked at the guy as threateningly as possible, but he had already turned away.

"I gotta go," said Jimbo. "Have fun."

"See ya," Billy said as he slipped in behind the wheel.

His first drive in his brand new car consisted of gunning the accelerator such that he reached thirty miles per hour before he was stopped by the left turn light on the corner. Upon turning he was impeded by a pair of boxy domestic sedans moving in parallel at about two miles per hour under the speed limit. Pulling out for another left, he entered the parking lot of his health club, tentatively maneuvering between potholes and into a parking space remote enough that he was unlikely to pick up a ding from a careless driver.

Inside, casually looking about for any familiar faces, and seeing none, he wondered if it would look silly to wear a button that said "Ask me about my new car!" He slipped into the locker room and changed clothes, emerged quickly, and found his rhythm, moving through his familiar workout routine, working up a glow, then a full sweat; moving from station to station in time to the canned techno backbeat emanating from the nasal sound system.

From the corner of his eye he was watching a strikingly beautiful Philippina-looking girl a couple of treadmills over. Her long pony-tail was swishing back and forth in time with her stride; her dark skin conspicuously offset by a bright, baby-blue spandex halter top. She was focused in on a rerun of *Cheers* playing on the TV in front of the line of treadmills.

Billy took a moment to appreciate the view and then casually stepped on to the treadmill next to her. She glanced at him and he gave her his warmest smile, which she did not return.

"You don't mind if a watch along with you, do you?" he asked, hoping for a reply of, "No, but I'd rather just go have sex right now." Instead, he just got a shake of the head.

Billy went to work. He needed to determine two things. First, the speed of her treadmill. It was easy to see it was set at a little over six miles per hour. Billy set his to just under six so he could be impressed with now fast she was running. Second, he needed to determine if there was anything shiny on the ring finger of her left hand. This was easier said than done as he had taken the treadmill to her right; the one to her left was occupied by a particularly intense power-walker in an oversized t-shirt that said *The Booty Don't Stop!*

Of course, it wasn't like a ring would stop him. The last time he approached a woman with a wedding ring at the gym, he asked if her husband worked out there. She said, "I'm not married. I just wear this to keep the assholes away." That would have been that last woman he slept with—Marlene excepted.

"It's hard to see that it's fake, isn't it?" he asked.

"What?" She removed her headphones.

"Oh, sorry. I said it's hard to imagine his hair is fake, isn't it?"

"Really? The bartender? The tall one?"

"Yeah, it's a hairpiece."

"How do you know? Is he, like, bald in the new ones, or something?"

"There are no new ones. It went off the air quite a few years ago."

"Oh. I don't watch classics too much."

The classics? uh-oh. Billy said, "Are you a student?"

"Yeah. A grad student," she replied, obviously on guard against being taken for a mere undergrad.

"What are you studying?"

"P-chem."

"Really? Wow. That's impressive." Billy had no idea what p-chem meant. "Masters?"

"Yeah."

"Going to go for your Ph.D.? I'm Billy, by the way."

"My parents want me to go to Med school, but I'm sick of school," she replied, conspicuously not reciprocating the introduction.

Billy smiled, thinking of a similar conversation with Jimbo. "I understand."

Her treadmill eased to a slow crawl. As she patted her neck and chest with a towel, Billy surreptitiously slowed his machine.

"I'm tired of living like a student," she said. "I want to get a decent place to live, and a nice car and things."

"I know what you mean." Billy remained in pursuit. "Nice stuff is good. I just picked up a nice new car. It's nice to be able to afford nice stuff."

"What did you get?"

"An Audi." Billy made his move. "Would you like to —"

"It was nice meeting you; I've got to get going."

"Yeah, maybe I'll see—" She disappeared into the

women's locker room.

After a short and feeble attempt to look unperturbed, Billy maneuvered through some shambling, jocky, basketball types to reach the men's locker room where he showered angrily.

••••

"No *you* are going to read to *me*."

"No, *you* read!"

"No."

"No, *you*."

"Missy, I am not playing a game. You need to read."

"Why?"

"Because you need to practice or you are going to fall behind in school."

"Why?"

The phone rang. "Missy, if you don't you'll forget everything you learned last year."

"Why?"

"Melissa Anne, stop doing that! Hello."

The instant Marlene turned away, Missy dashed off and plopped down in front of the TV.

"What do you mean 'change of plan?' Why...I can't just change—" Marlene cradled the phone between her chin and shoulder and set her hands firmly on her hips.

"Mommy the TV won't work!"

"Not now Missy! I'm talking to your father. You can't keep doing this. Yes you do! You always—" Her shoulders slumped in resignation.

"Mommy!"

"Sure you will. Whatever you say. Do you...Do you want to talk to her? Missy, come talk to your father!"

"Mommy the TV won't work! I keep telling you but you won't help!"

"Missy, you're not supposed to be watching TV, you're supposed to be reading. Come talk to your father."

"No! I want to watch TV!"

"Sorry...OK...OK...fine...bye." The hostile snap of the phone into its cradle caused Skippy, the hyperactive beagle, to jump and yip.

"Mommy!"

"Missy stop screeching!"

"But why won't you help me!"

The phone rang again. "Hello...yes...What do you mean 'change in plan'?" Marlene's grip on the handset tightened as she closed her eyes in frustration.

"Help me, Mommy!"

"Missy, be quiet, it's work. Eight AM? I can't make it. That's when I drop Missy."

"Mommy!"

"Can't someone else...what about Jake or Jim or... Chad, look, what would you do if I was dead? How would you handle it if I was dead? Handle it that way. Jesus!"

"Help me! Mommy!"

"Missy, shut up! Look, I can't just change plans ... Chad... Chad...then why can't everyone else be there when I...no, no... alright...alright...I'll try...bye." Another phone snap. Another jump from Skippy.

Missy was bawling hysterically.

Marlene walked over to her, knelt down in front of her and gently said, "Missy, why do you have to scream like that?"

"Because I was trying to turn on the Cartoon Channel and it kept being wrong and no matter what I did it wouldn't work and you wouldn't help me!"

"Missy, you're supposed to be reading."

"I don't want to read! I want to watch the Cartoon Channel but the TV wouldn't work and you wouldn't help me!" Missy threw the remote on the floor and resumed bawling.

"Maybe it would be better if you just went to bed."

"Nooo!" The bawling amplified.

The phone rang again.

"Hello...What? What do you mean 'change in plan'?"

••••

For the moment, the best use of the Audi seemed to be to circle the block a few times and hope a space on the street opened up, rather than park in the structure. The Audi came through for him on the third circumnavigation and he slid easily into a spot directly in front of Duncan McFunkin's, the single most contrived fake Irish-pub in the Western Hemisphere. As he entered, he noticed a plaque on the wall indicating that the local paper had declared Duncan McFunkin's to be "The Hottest Pick-up Spot in Town." Appropriate, since years of experience had taught him the importance of getting back on the proverbial horse straight away.

Billy made his way to the bar and ordered a Guinness. He garnered a smile of recognition from the bartender.

"What's the good word, Bud?" the bartender asked, coyly noncommittal on the appellation.

"I'm still kickin'," Billy replied deftly.

The bartender gave him a practiced wink. "That's all the counts, eh?" he said thoughtlessly and moved off.

Billy scanned the room; it was a moderately busy evening. He estimated that there were about seventy-five patrons, of which about fifteen were women, of which maybe seven were not obviously attached to someone.

Of those seven, four were together in a circle and from his vantage point he could see that at least two of the quartet had wedding rings. Billy considered approaching them, but decorum meant he would have to buy a round for all of them and when combined with the wedding ring uncertainty factor it seemed like a low percentage play.

Two more of the seven were engaged in a very animated conversation with each other. Normally that would be a plus as it's easier to step into an existing conversation than start from scratch, but there was a good deal of negative body language—head shaking, tightening fists and what looked to be the vestiges of tears. Drama. Next, please.

The remaining unattached woman at the Hottest

Pick-up Spot in Town was drinking a glass of red wine and checking messages on her Blackberry. She occasionally looked up, not to see who was looking, but lost in thought, then immediately returned to her email. Billy suspected she was probably there to make herself available in theory, but so afraid of the possibility of actually meeting someone that she was occupying herself anti-socially and so prepping herself to fail at the task but take comfort in the effort. The act wouldn't fool Billy. Her obvious emotional struggle would play into his finely-honed relaxed sincerity. She was the target. She looked to be late-twenties, but dressed older, more professionally. No obvious sense of underlying body shape to judge as yet. Nice eyes. Good posture. A fair horse to get back on. But as soon as Billy shifted his weight off the barstool, a man in a turtleneck and sport coat appeared from behind her and gave her a familiar kiss before taking the seat next to her.

Billy exhaled deeply and contemplated what was left of his Guinness. Much longer and it would be too warm and too flat to drink. He downed it.

Billy looked around the bar again. It had filled up and there was a line of would be revelers waiting outside the door—overwhelmingly male; all in $200 jeans and untucked, striped button down shirts. His eye caught his own image in the mirror behind the bar. Some time ago, he had read an article in a glossy men's magazine about how important it was for an unattached man in a bar to be able to look 'alone, but not lonely.'

He exhaled again, more deeply, and flipped open his cell phone and called Marlene. "Hi, it's me. There's been a change in plan—"

Billy had to hold the phone away from his ear for a moment. When the shouting stopped, he said, "I mean, I'm going to move in with you."

August 31

Someone needed to adjust the brightness. The sun radiated a blinding, halogen glare in the near total lack of shade. The houses all had blinding white trim. The cars were waxed to a blinding sheen. Even the streets and sidewalks were blindingly clean.

By design, the side streets meandered just enough to provide the character of an organic neighborhood. The houses were newly built within the couple of years; all variations on a three bedroom, two-and-a-half bath, attached two car garage theme. The mere sprouts that passed for trees on the front lawns filled Billy with trepidation, like Cary Grant in *North by Northwest* about to encounter mortal terror in the great wide-open.

Marlene and Missy greeted him with hugs. Skippy jumped up and down and howled like a banshee. Missy promptly went back to shoveling gooey macaroni and cheese into her face from a precarious kneeling position on the edge of her chair while Skippy alternately nipped at his heals and dodged his footsteps.

"Do you need help getting the rest of your stuff out of your car?" Marlene asked.

"This is all I brought," Billy said, looking down at his single carry-on bag.

"Oh."

"I figured I'd move little by little—I'll stop by after work and get some more each day."

"Well, why don't you take that upstairs."

"Mommy, can Billy sleep in my room?"

"There's only one bed in your room, sweetie."

"Is he going to sleep on the couch?"

Billy had been dreading this moment. He chose to keep his mouth shut.

"Sweetie, Billy's going to sleep in my room."

"But there's only one bed in your room."

"Honey, Billy and I are going to sleep in the same bed," Marlene said with a maternal weightiness.

"Are you going to get married?"

Billy wondered how bad this was going to get.

"Honey, we're just going to see how this works out."

"Where's he going to go to the bathroom?"

"Out back behind the garage," Marlene deadpanned.

"No he's not," Missy giggled, and turned her attention back to her macaroni and cheese.

Billy kissed Missy on the top of her head, gave Marlene a look of admiration and took his bag up to the bedroom.

The Van Gogh sunflower and Monet water-lilies

stood in fearful contrast to the art-deco posters that decorated his bedroom at home. *At home.* The bed —queen-sized versus his king—was made, which heightened his consternation.

It hadn't occurred to him to ask where he should put his stuff; there were no empty drawers in the dresser. He could have made some space in the walk-in closet, but was afraid to move anything, suspecting there may be some secret, unwritten rules about closet contents known only to women, which would put him on the receiving end of a what-were-you-thinking look later that evening. He settled for leaving his carry-on unopened in a remote corner of the room and went back downstairs.

On the bottom stair, Billy stopped dead. Missy was talking to an adolescent girl. She had straight brown hair pulled back behind her ears, a slightly pudgy turned up nose and a defiant pout to her lips. Her features were not glamorously pretty, but fresh and natural, and her skin was perfect (blindingly perfect). She wore a lipstick-red, form fitting V-neck t-shirt with a pair of faded blue jeans, between which an inch-wide band of sub-navel flesh was bared. With great effort, Billy did not evaluate her breasts. She looked to be about seventeen and made Billy feel as dirty as he had ever felt.

She started to look up and Billy quickly shifted his eyes to Missy and then back to her.

"Hi, I'm Billy."

Missy jumped up and took Billy's hand and led him over to the girl. She looked up at Billy with clear sienna-brown eyes.

"This is Jenna, she's my babysitter, expect that I'm not really a baby," Missy declared with precocious grace. "Jenna, this is Billy. He's going to be sleeping in my Mom's room, but they're not getting married, they're just working it out."

Billy and Jenna laughed nervously.

"Nice to meet you," Jenna said. Three perfectly random locks of hair were loosely dancing on her forehead. On the front of her shirt were the words *Chicks Rule*.

Billy was mortified. He desperately did not want to give consideration to what the proper adjective might be, but "ample" was the instant word association. "You, too," he said.

"I see you've met," Marlene said, returning from a phone call.

"Your daughter was kind enough to introduce us," Billy replied.

Marlene handed Jenna some cash which she folded and put into her front pocket. Billy stole a glance at her hand as it slid down her thigh to seat the bills deeply.

"Jenna is Dora and Dick's daughter," Marlene said.

"Really? Then you must be the one Jimbo is always talking about."

Jenna brightened. "You know Jim?"

"Sure. I just bought an Audi; he's my connection. He's the man."

"Yeah, he is."

"Will he be around for the block party?" Marlene asked.

Billy's brow furrowed.

"Maybe. He's not sure," replied Jenna.

"What block party?" asked Billy.

"This Friday," Marlene explained tersely. "What about your Mom?"

"I think so. She's still playing, like, 'I don't really belong' and 'I don't live there anymore' and 'I haven't been invited.'"

"Oh, I'll call her. She'll come around," Marlene said. "She just needs to be wanted."

"I know," said Jenna with a smile.

"So your Mom and Dad get along OK?" Billy asked, then instantly feared it was inappropriate.

"Oh yeah. They're both too repressed to be blatantly hostile."

Billy smiled. The girl was sharp, too.

••••

After saying goodnight to Marlene, Jenna was overcome with her usual anxious depression about going home. She strolled particularly slowly, in the middle of the street, down the block to her house. She had nothing to talk about with her Dad. All he ever did was ask about her *future*. What are your plans? Have you thought about college? What you decide now will determine your *future*. Screw that, it's just life. It just happens, what's the point of planning? He didn't know how to talk to her. His only style of communication was the instructional lecture. He was, after all, an *educator*. Well, if he was so smart how come he was as fucked up as everyone else? Her mom was the opposite; she just made pointless small talk, or cried, and that just made Jenna angry—like she was supposed to sit there while her Mom cried for no reason, but if she left it just made it worse.

Things were much better when she had to babysit. She could hang out at school for a while or just meet up with Jim somewhere until she had to go to Marlene's so that it would be late when she got home and could go right to bed. She always liked to get there early because she could talk to Marlene, woman to woman. Marlene always seemed to have everything under control, like when she told her she was pretty sure Jim wanted to have sex and Marlene didn't freak out or lecture her or anything, she just asked, "So are you going to sleep with him?" just like she was talking to one of her other girlfriends.

Her mom was one of Marlene's girlfriends, she suddenly remembered. She needed to be careful because as close as she was to Marlene, adults had this like secret code that made them do stuff like blab to each other in the children's best interest. Would Marlene have told her about Jim wanting sex? No. If she had told, then her mom would have called and broken into tears unprompted, but the last time they spoke, when Jenna made one of her perfunctory visits for dinner and a silent hour of watching TV, there was no indication she had received any dish from Marlene, just a good fifteen minutes of talk about diet and calories before she started crying.

Now she felt fat. Her father was considerably overweight, her mom less so but still heavy. Though she habitually went around with an exposed midriff, her stomach wasn't all flat like some of her friends. Her boobs were pretty good, she knew, but her legs—not so much. She was obsessively conscious of how and when she could sit so as not to show the folds on her sides or spread to her thighs. Of course, Jim always told her she was beautiful, which she knew wasn't so; it was probably that he wanted sex, but it was very sweet of him anyway.

Not like most of the other boys she knew who were always putting down their girlfriends.

The boys she knew were all pretty lame. They were always trying to prove they could do something or talking themselves up, except it was all talk. But Jim didn't do much of that, except when he talked about cool cars and how fun it is to drive fast in them and then talking about these tiny differences in how fast they were or something about tires. She figured all cars do is pollute the air so she just wanted a small one, maybe a hybrid, or maybe a little convertible, but that might be cold in the winter.

Reaching for the doorknob, her greatest fear was that her father would want to have a "connection session"—a good hour or so of forced conversation to make sure "the lines of communication were open." That meant she would have to come up with roughly thirty minutes of true, or unverifiably false, parenting manual-worthy teenager troubles so that he would believe she was healthy and only concerned with the innocent and completely normal conflicts of adolescence, when her real concern was whether to take up smoking because her friend Denise did one summer and came back to school with a tiny waist. That, and whether to have sex with Jim. If it wasn't for her own existence, she would have pegged her dad as a virgin.

She entered as quietly as possible but managed only a few steps towards her room when her father called to her. She winced, flashing back to the time they had The Talk (her mother couldn't bring herself to do it). It was only recently that she had come to terms with hearing the words "your vagina" come out of her father's mouth. Maybe she'd be lucky and it would only be something stupid this time, like when he suggested she could call him by his first name if she wanted. She didn't want to call her father Dick in anything but anger.

"Hi, Honey. Where've you been?" asked Dick, with an exactingly-measured friendliness.

"I was at Denise's, then Marlene's. Getting paid." She casually edged closer to the stairs.

Dick's head bobbed as he glanced out the window and turned the porch light on then back off, as if to test it. "Oh. Say, is your friend Jim going to be coming to the block party?"

"I don't know." Jenna turned away and focused on slipping her sandals off and examining them.

"OK." Dick slid his hands in his pockets and rocked on his toes. "Well—"

"Well, I'm going to get some stuff done," said Jenna, darting hastily upstairs without waiting for a reply.

••••

Lying awake at three-thirty, Billy was thinking about sex, and not in the usual naked-supermodels-pillow-fight way. The consternation of Missy's probing questions about bed-sharing and the appearance of the Lolita in the *Chicks Rule* t-shirt had Billy so intimidated that Marlene was the recipient of what might have been his most timid love-making effort since adolescence. Afterward, she declared it to have been "sweet," set her alarm, turned over and went to sleep. An inauspicious start to shared life.

At one minute to six, Skippy jumped on Billy's testicles.

"OW!! Son of a...OW!!"

Marlene woke with a start, and upon seeing Billy

clutching his groin and Skippy cowering in the corner began laughing hysterically.

"STUPID GODDAM DOG!"

The alarm went off.

Billy whipped a pillow at Skippy.

Skippy urinated in fear and shame.

Marlene said "Oh, Skippy," and leapt to action to prevent carpet staining.

"Jesus Christ!" Billy said through clenched teeth, huddled into a little ball of pain.

"MOMMY!" Missy called from her bedroom.

Billy longed for the clock to say two minutes of six again. He spent the remainder of the day in a mild daze of weary confusion. He forgot to mention his new Audi to anyone at work. Afterward, he stopped back at his condo and filled a garment bag with enough clothes to get him through the week. Taking a moment to relax, he slouched down in his recliner and turned on ESPN.

Even with the TV on and the downtown noise just outside the window, it still seemed quieter than the suburbs. Billy sat silently processing the day until he realized he was watching figure skating. He rose, and with his garment bag slung over his shoulder, gathered his mail on the way out, leaving a just arrived copy of Men's Journal for the next time he had a few minutes alone. All the way to Marlene's house he obeyed the speed limit.

PART 2

Plans Are Best Laid

September 3

Billy raised his hand as a shield against the late-afternoon sun. Through the sparkling clear, streak-free, upstairs bedroom window he could see the entire block party unfolding, as if he were watching The Sims on autopilot. Missy was playing with a gaggle of other children in the little playground. She called to the other kids and ran in circles with them. After a brief discussion about what manic action to take next a decision was made on a basis only a 6-year-old could understand, then more chaotic scurrying ensued—all done with a perfect unselfconscious purity. Marlene was out of her scope of attention, but she was well within Marlene's, about twenty yards away and stealing glances at Missy every few seconds.

Marlene was like a modern image of Jackie O. with her easy-going, casual elegance, dark hair and broad smile. Always composed, but never stiff, she was clearly the alpha female of the neighborhood. She stared up at the window where Billy was standing, leaving Billy unsure of whether she could see him through the glare. Billy smiled and waved just in case, but she turned away.

The fellow in the sweater had to be Dick. He had heard plenty of degrading stories about Dick, all told with warnings that they were never to be repeated, indicating that although he was the butt of jokes, he was still a member of clique and worthy of sparing any pain.

Dick was grilling didactically. Billy had never realized it was possible to grill didactically, but Dick was doing it—keeping up a running lecture on the theory and practice of grilling for everyone who stepped up for a burger or a bratwurst, and, when no one was around, administering the same lecture to the meat itself through body language and countenance. He looked like nothing so much as a walrus in both body shape and facial design—sagging jowls, sagacious eyes, and thick Fu Manchu style mustache that seemed to pull his cheeks even lower. Clad in a cardigan, in the middle of summer, along with shorts and sandals over white socks, he was every teenager's worst nightmare of a father —imagine your friends actually *seeing* him. Poor Jenna had this misery compounded by having him as a teacher at her high school. It was almost certainly a searing trauma that would provide some future therapist with a time-share in Cabo.

Jenna and Jimbo were sitting together on the steps of her porch, on the outskirts of the multitude, sipping Diet Cokes and watching diffidently, occasionally sharing a whispered critique so smarmy that Billy could practically smell it from afar. Billy was never less than awed at how effortless it was for women to look beautiful. They seemed to know exactly how to sit to emphasize their figures, how to smile with their moist lips just slightly apart, how to flip their hair back, how to be so powerfully enrapturing. Even at age seventeen and born of a walrus, Jenna had this ability. He felt dirty again and forced himself to look off.

Scanning the crowd he spotted Jenna's mom (Dick's ex) Dora, looking a bit puffy and smiling nervously. She had positioned herself at the edge of the activity, a solo lioness hoping to slip stealthily into the pride. Like her ex-husband, she was one who came in for unrepeatable criticism; perhaps a bit more sympathetic in her case. She had something of a deer-in-the-headlights look about her, laughing readily and working hard to keep conversations genial and superficial. Lacking any sense of subtlety, skepticism, or absurdity, she made her bones solely on conventions of civility and kindness. Jenna had a double whammy of parent poison—her father was embarrassment incarnate and her mother was congenitally incapable of irony.

Dora took to busying herself rearranging various plastic utensils, plates and condiments on one of the large picnic tables. Flip stepped up to the table and said something that made Dora's nervous smile grow broader and more nervous. Flip was about as much a good ol' suburban American male as it was possible to be: a former high school jock whose hair was starting to thin and whose stomach was exploring new territory. He was still jabbering with

Dora as he sampled the potato salad directly from the serving spoon and thoughtlessly replaced it. Dora just kept her smile and replaced the serving spoon as non-judgmentally as possible.

Flip's wife, Pammy, was less forgiving. She stepped up behind him, grabbed his arm and spun him around to chastise him to his face. Billy was amused at the sight of tiny little Pammy, at least a foot shorter than Flip and not more than a hundred and ten pounds in hiking boots, cowing Flip so thoroughly that his shoulders stooped and his head hung. As he sulked off, Pammy turned to Dora and just shook her head. Dora laughed it off nervously. Pammy had a definite hint of cuteness about her, lingering from her youth, though she had become a bit bottom heavy. Billy expected she was one of the fun girls in whatever circle she happened to inhabit. Acerbic and gregarious; she was likely the one who kept things entertaining wherever she went. For a moment he was disappointed that she had not seen fit to flirt with him on the sly, then he remembered they were all adults.

Flip made his way over to the grill. Dick had just opened a beer and, before he even took a sip, began explain the finer points of controlling the heat of the coals to Flip. Flip suddenly interrupted and pointed at something off in the distance. When Dick's attention was turned, he swapped his empty beer bottle for Dick's full one. Dick looked back and Flip just shrugged and walked off. Dick did a stunned double take when he tipped the bottle to his lips.

Billy chuckled. His attention turned back to Marlene; she was talking to Sarah. Did she know that Sarah and Billy had a brief fling a couple years back? He would tell her if asked, he vowed, but why risk an adverse reaction. She probably knew. Sarah was part of the little foursome of friends; no doubt they had been through each other's sexual history in mortifying detail, liberally punctuated with snide comments and degrading giggles. Women are pigs.

Except it wouldn't be like Sarah to say anything without a good cause. She would reason that no good would come of it and she shouldn't accept the negativity of bringing it up just out of spite. Not a vindictive bone in her slender body. Not a greedy one or a selfish one or a conceited one either. That was the problem; Billy always felt guilty whenever he exposed one of his less righteous personality traits to her. That dynamic was redefined in casual conversation as "things just didn't work out." Her inner calm and penchant for self-reflection didn't extend to the bedroom, Billy reminisced. Being a yoga instructor really paid off when it came to... Jesus Christ! Could he not go five minutes without thinking of sex? Was he forty or eighteen?

Billy breathed deeply. It was quite a cast of characters out on the suburban veldt. He would hate to be a novelist and have to keep track of them all. Apprehensively, he walked down the stairs, out the door, and into the breach.

••••

The sun walloped Billy the instant he stepped out the door. He stepped back inside to get his sunglasses and baseball cap. Marlene winked at him as he crossed the street to the grill.

"You must be Billy," called Dick as he offered an oven-mitted hand. "Oh, sorry—heh-heh."

"And you're Jenna's father, right?"

"Oh, heh-heh, you notice the resemblance?"

"The only resemblance between you and your

daughter is your address," Flip interrupted, slapping Dick on the back and winking at Billy. Billy made note of the whole winking thing as a possible social norm.

"Oh, heh-heh," responded Dick. "How 'bout a brat, Billy? This one is just about perfect—see the even browning. The trick is to give 'em a quarter turn at decreasing intervals. Now, you see this one here, well, heh-heh, it cooked too slow so by the time the outside was brown the interior was over cooked—dry. Heat was too low at the—"

"Dick, the wienermeister," offered Flip.

"—whereas these over here browned too quickly. What happened was the wind shifted and altered the hot spots on the grill."

Billy was momentarily dumbfounded. "Uh, you must do a lot of grilling."

"My first time, actually."

Flip snorted.

A screen door slammed in the distance, filling one of those unlikely moments of silence that seem to sporadically wash over crowds. All eyes turned.

A large, awkward, amorphous creature with long unkempt hair and high-water pants stepped out of a house about half-way down the block.

"Freak alert," announced Flip.

Presently, the adults caught themselves staring and downshifted to taking furtive glances, leaving the blatant staring to the children. Dick scowled but kept his attention on the grill. Pammy slipped in beside Flip and they alternated their furtive glances like a practiced married couple.

Jenna, who had made her way to the grill to load up a couple of paper plates for her and Jimbo, adopted an ironic grin. "Looks like your friend is coming by," she smart-mouthed to her father.

The creature was steadily making way to the grill, employing a thick, robotic shuffle for locomotion.

Dick mumbled, "Profiteering bastard."

The creature made his final approach of the grill. With an unnatural, painted-on smile, he cocked an elbow and gave a stilted wave in an effort to dispel any hostility. Billy couldn't fathom why there was such an electric undercurrent. He put Billy in mind of nothing more than an adult version of a chubby high school geek; an aging practitioner of Dungeons and Dragons.

The creature stood for a moment at the grill, his smile unwavering. After a few seconds of silence, he pointed to the grill and said, "Do you suppose I could get a couple of those bratwursts?"

"You want two?" Dick replied sternly.

"Yeah." The inscrutable smile remained unchanged.

Pammy and Flip exchanged looks. Dora had moved silently into the core of the group and was getting a hushed update on the situation from Marlene. Jenna stood nearby, still grinning the grin of a supercilious seventeen-year-old; the grin of an adolescent confronted with the limitless folly of grown-ups.

Slowly—avoiding eye contact—Dick lifted a paper plate with two bratwurst just as Jenna said, "Oh look, there's Mom." Dick looked up and the brats tumbled into the dirt.

Dora waved hello. Dick spat a mild profanity. Jenna giggled. The creature's smile did not waiver.

Dick stared balefully at the creature then began preparing another two brats. Billy had to do something to quell his mischievous need to get in on this, whatever it was. He extended a hand. "Hi. I'm Billy."

The creature appeared taken by surprise, as if this was a new experience. He tentatively shook Billy's hand saying, "I'm Otto."

Based on the group reaction, Billy would have estimated Otto to be a convicted child molester; one of those guys who, upon parole from the big house, was under judicial order to go door-to-door through the neighborhood and tell everyone he was a sex offender. Thus, Billy asked, "So what do you do, Otto?" with a bit of trepidation.

"Well," Otto replied with a deep exhale. "I guess you would call me a collector; an entrepreneur of a sort."

Dick dropped the brats again. Flip snorted. Dick spat a slightly less mild profanity. Otto kept smiling.

"That's interesting," Billy pursued. "What do you collect?"

"That's a big question. I collect and sell anything people will buy."

"Really? What sorts of things?"

"Oh, this and that; the stuff of popular interest at the moment."

"So, what is of popular interest at this moment."

"Well, one can never be certain, but there are indications."

Billy deemed Otto to be an obnoxious, fat-ass, loser twit. Dick finally completed the bratwurst hand-off to Otto, who did nothing to acknowledge the effort. He gave an affected nod to Billy and walked stiffly away, wolfing down the brats.

Once Otto was out of earshot, Billy asked, "What the hell was that?"

"The neighborhood freak show," Flip replied.

"I hate that S.O.B.," Dick offered.

Jenna giggled again. She rested her hand on her bosom, which was covered in an electric blue v-neck t-shirt that said *Previously Owned*. Billy winced and turned away.

Dick glared at her sternly. "We need some more buns. Jenna would you run to the store and get some?"

"We wouldn't need 'em if you didn't spaz out and start fertilizing the lawn with them. Geez."

"What's wrong with that guy," Billy asked.

"He's a thief," replied Dick. "Nothing more, nothing less. A greedy, opportunistic, reactionary, thief."

"Oh, Dad, he didn't steal. You agreed to the price."

"Jenna, would you please go to the store to get more buns?"

Jenna just rolled her smarmy, seventeen-year-old eyes.

"What would you call it," Dick asked Billy, "if you prey on the innocent, people who don't have inside information? He's no better than those corrupt CEOs who do all the insider trading."

"Please," said Jenna.

"Jenna," Dick exasperated.

Billy presumed they must have been business partners in a deal that went bad. Billy was wrong. Jenna took pleasure in setting the record straight. "He bought some old albums—you know the old vinyl kind with the little hole in the middle—off Dad at a garage sale for a buck a piece. Turns out a couple of them were worth over two-hundred dollars."

"Oh, more than that. I found out when I saw he was selling them on eBay. The bidding was up to two-fifty when I caught him. Hell, I tried to be diplomatic. I suggested the fair thing to do would be to split whatever he got. He just grins and says, 'A deal is a deal.' Bastard. Stood there grinning, knowing he had cheated me and there was nothing I could do about it. See what I mean about corrupt? Cheat 'em just because you can. Like some kind of robber baron."

"Wow," exclaimed Billy, although if pressed he probably would have agreed with Otto in principle. And Dick seemed to take a veiled, morally righteous relish in his victimization.

Marlene and Dora stepped up looking for the scoop. Flip filled them in on the recent events, adding a highly stylized demonstration of Dick dropping the bratwursts. Twice.

"Then we heard the legend of the Great Garage Sale Robbery," Jenna added.

"Oh dear," said Dora.

"Yes: Oh dear," Dick added defensively.

Dora tossed him a menacing look.

Marlene stepped in. "Some people look at life as a sum of debits and credits," she said in polite sympathy.

"Yeah," said Flip. "Even a lousy twelve-sixty-seven a month."

"What's that about?" asked Billy.

Jenna touched Billy on the arm, which alarmed him in so many ways, and said, "Now we'll hear about the Great Fountain Maintenance Scandal."

"Jenna," Dora chastised.

Flip took the floor. "See the central island there in the middle of the cul-de-sac? Kind of dull isn't it —just a few shrubs, a wooden bench, that's about it. It could have been great. It could have been beautiful. We had a plan to put a fountain there— very nice faux marble, patterned after a famous one in Venice..."

"Florence," Pammy corrected.

"...or maybe Florence. Had a landscape firm all

set up to do some nice horticulture. It was something for the whole neighborhood, you know? Increase property values, and such. Thing is, we had to make arrangements with the city—get them to run water to it, and there were licenses, and maintenance arrangements and so forth. I made all the arrangements—and it was a total bureaucratic nightmare pain in the ass, let me tell you."

"Seriously," Pammy whispered to Dora, "we had no sex while this was going on."

"I even took two sick days just so I could corner the right paper-hanging pinheads at City Hall to get everything signed and delivered. So what it all comes down to is I find a way that everyone with property adjacent to the cul-de-sac has to pay twelve sixty-seven a month for this—it gets added right into your property tax bill, no hassle, all you gotta do is agree to it. One by one everyone agrees, no hesitation, except that fu—"

"Hey, there's kids here!" shouted a small, pug-nosed, blonde child.

"Shaadup!" snapped Flip, wielding the back of his hand. "—that freakin' Neanderthal, Otto. Lard-ass probably spends more than that on bacon double cheeseburgers every day, but he refuses. Can't see the benefit, he says. So I go back around and try to explain to everyone that since that dimwitted troll refuses, the cost goes up to thirteen ninety-four. Of course, no one will do it. They want to know why they should pay more when the freak show is getting off for free. Asshole."

"Um..." declared Billy. Again, although he thought it was rather chincy, he could see Otto's side. He had no interest in the fountains and probably didn't really care all that much how the neighborhood looked, why should he pay extra every month? But, Billy reminded himself, this is a different world—a green, neighborly world. Otto had clearly violated more than one sacrosanct precept of suburban communalism.

Dora instantly tried to sympathize with the enemy. "Well, for someone to be like that, in this nice neighborhood, he must have had some bad experiences in his life."

Flip sneered. "Like what, the 7-11 ran out of Little Debbies?"

Dora persevered. "He's obviously not very socially adept. Being anti-social is just a defense mechanism."

"My ass," snorted Dick. Dora hit him with a look women reserve for their ex-husbands. Everyone held their breath.

Dick sheepishly explained, "It's just that the obvious reason for everything he does is money. He's a pure materialist. The worst kind of moneygrubber. He judges everything by how it affects his wallet. 'Collector' he calls himself—you see? He preys on the worst instincts of people. Baseball cards, figurines, toys, you name it—he corners the market and waits for the price to rise, then he's all over eBay selling it for three times the price. Or more. He's no better than any of those Wall Street CEO crooks. He screws the little guy, the average citizen, to line his pockets. He's a consumer raping capitalist, that's all he is. I bet he's even a Republican."

"Oh gawd!" cried Jenna.

Again, Billy didn't see the evil. Surely, he wasn't putting a gun to anyone's head to do business with him. And judging from the way he dressed, his pocket linings were probably full of holes, not gold. Not only that, Billy had known a couple of Republicans and found them to be pretty much just like normal people.

"Jenna, didn't I ask you to go to the store?"

"You know, I bet he's got a pile of Tori Tornados in his basement."

On cue, a pack of striplings appeared, Missy among them, howling about someone having Tori Tornado.

Marlene reasoned with them, "No one has Tori Tornado, we were just talking."

Unwilling to accept the word of a Mom not their own, three pug-nosed blonde boy-children of varying size beset Pammy with the same question. Not as well behaved as Missy, they kept screeching 'Who? Who?' like a nest full of owl chicks. Flip told them to "Shut up and go play!" which they did, with a certain resigned dignity.

"You see? I bet he's all over eBay with those things just before the holidays."

As if to validate the attraction focused on him, Otto's garage door opened and a non-descript, weather-worn, domestic sedan backed out. It slithered slowly, and quite clumsily, around the makeshift barricades set up to keep traffic out for the block party. Just as it had almost completed the gauntlet, it sideswiped a pair of garbage cans at the end of Flip's driveway. Either not noticing or pretending not to, Otto continued on out of the neighborhood.

"That bastard," spat Flip.

"That bastard," mimicked the pug-nosed blond child at his knee.

Flip slapped him on the head. "Hey! I don't want to hear that kind of language again. Go pick up those trash cans!"

The child did no such thing.

"Did you see that? Did you see that?" Flip asked in fervent indignation.

"Let's put him in stocks and throw this macaroni salad at him. And this cheese dip too," Jenna laughed.

"Jenna! That's enough attitude." Dora snapped. She didn't want Pammy to take offense at Jenna belittling her husband. Pammy didn't notice really, since she wrote the book on belittling her husband.

"Jenna. Would you please go to the store?" Dick asked sternly and distinctively. "This is the fourth time I've asked."

"I guess you need to learn when to quit." Jenna was on a rebellious teenage hot streak now.

"Jenna!" Dora snapped.

Dick drew himself up to full height in preparation for a textbook boundary definition lecture, when Billy interrupted. "Here," he said, holding out the keys to his Audi. "You can take my car. Let Jimbo drive."

Jenna looked at him suspiciously. Billy winked at her and instantly realized he had used an I-want-to-see-you-naked wink instead of the hey-we're-all-good-suburbanites wink he had seen earlier. Oh no! Did she see it? Did anyone else? Oh no!

Jenna smiled a smile that was simultaneously innocent and sexual. "Thanks," she said, snatching the keys and darting off.

Everyone else stared slackjawed at Billy.

Oh Jesus Christ no! It was truly an innocent mistake. Really it was—Freud be damned. Did that smile mean she got the wrong message, or the right message for the wrong reason, or the wrong message for the right reason? Oh no! *A forty year-old man was arrested today for blatantly flirting with a seventeen year-old girl in a quiet suburban subdivision in front of her parents and neighbors. He was sentenced to visit each home in a half-mile radius and inform the residents that he was nothing but an oversexed man-child who was destined for an old age of isolation and pornography.* He should have just avoided her entirely as soon as she made him feel so... He should have averted his eyes and walked away when she was near.

Breath held, he turned to face his fate. Pammy was shaking her head, stunned. Flip's jaw was down around his belly-button. Dick dropped more brats and didn't even notice. Marlene's hand was over her mouth in shock.

"What the hell was that!?" cried Dick. "Did I just see what I think I saw?"

One of the women said "Oh. My. God."

"Jesus H. Christ on a bike!" Flip added.

Almost panting in fear of this potential lynch mob, Billy could only muster a mildly defensive "Wha?"

Marlene said, "Darling, do you realize you just gave

your car keys to a teenager."

Flip amplified the sentiment. "Are you insane? Are you an insane man? Is that your problem?"

"Are you an insane man? Is that your problem?" mimicked a little blonde child at Flip's knee, who deftly dodged the resulting swat.

....

Jimbo had a Volkswagen, but not a Beetle; it was one of those little hatchbacks. He got it shortly after he started working for the Audi/VW dealer. Jenna remembered because it was exactly one week and four days after they started going out, which she defined as the day they first kissed when they were hanging out behind the school on a Sunday afternoon with Laurie and Scott and Jeanie and Kurt and they were all coupled up so it was just sort of expected that she would make out with Jim.

She had liked Jim for a while, sort of, not like a serious crush or anything but he was a cute guy, maybe a borderline hottie, but she couldn't stand that everyone called him Jimbo. It was so vulgar, like he was some kind of hillbilly or something.

The Audi was nice car but she didn't really care about cars. Billy seemed like a nice guy but how weird was it to lend his car out like that?

"Would you be careful?" Jimbo snapped.

"What? I'm just finding 97.3."

"You don't know what buttons to press, you could screw something up."

"Relax. Geez, I'm just changing the station. It's a radio. I can work a radio."

"But he'll know we messed with it."

"So?"

"I want make sure he gets it back just like it was."

"Is that why you're driving, like, thirty below the speed limit?"

"I'm not driving thirty below the speed limit. That would be five miles per hour. I'm not driving five miles per hour."

"True. You'd have to speed up."

Jenna was silently impressed with how responsible

he was. The first time they went out he took her to a two-dollar old-movie matinee—*Legally Blonde* —which was a good movie, but she had to drive because his Mom needed their car because they only had one, so she borrowed her Mom's car, which was good because if her mom asked any stupid questions about where she was going and what she was doing she could act indignant and her mom would back off, unlike her Dad who would have taken the opportunity to lecture her about automotive safety then pat himself on the back for being a concerned parent.

She knew Jim felt embarrassed about her having to drive because the next week he got a job at the VW/ Audi dealer and bought the VW hatchback off the lot, which he kept nice even though it had like five million miles on it. The next time they went out he made it absolutely clear that the car was his so they didn't have to ask for permission anymore. Ever. Jenna liked the taste of independence and control; to come and go as she pleased. She also liked that he was more dependable and reserved than her—not that she was really wild or anything, like some of her girlfriends at school who just thought life was a big reality TV show or something. And she liked how feminine and powerful it made her feel that he would step out of his skin to be alone with her.

"Why don't you drive by the school?" she asked coyly.

"It's out of the way."

"Yeah, by like, two blocks."

Jimbo looked dubious.

"Please," she said, lightly pulling her hair behind her ear.

"OK, we can drive by but we can't stop."

"We don't have to; you're driving slow enough that anyone we see can just walk along side."

Passing the school, Jenna craned and swiveled her neck to see who happened to be loitering. At the sight of a couple of chatting girls she instructed Jim to circle toward them. Jim complied, sighing audibly. Jenna and the two girls began a coded conversation.

"Hey."

"Hey. Cool car."

"Yeah."

"Yeah. So what up?"

"Nothin'."

"Yeah."

"What about you?"

"Nothin'. Seein' who's going."

"To who?"

"Danger."

"Oh, derp."

"Who's car?"

"Mine."

"Oh, yeah, right."

"It belongs to a guy I know," Jimbo interjected, employing a distasteful complete sentence.

"So, what up?"

"Lame block party. So who's around?"

"Cody, Max, those jerks," the girl indicated a group of four boys jostling and shambling in their direction.

Jimbo instantly identified them as the gravest threat

to anyone trying to avoid trouble: a pack of bored teenage boys. "Well, we gotta go," he quickly announced. "See ya."

"What are you doing?" Jenna cried.

"That's trouble," Jimbo said, indicating the boys.

"Oh please, they're just a bunch of jerks."

As they drove away, the boys gave a short chase then stopped, out of breath, and extended their middle fingers. The girls they had been talking to shouted something unintelligible at the boys who responded by re-targeting their fingers at the girls.

"I am totally sure!" Jenna declared. "Are you afraid of those idiots?"

"I'm afraid they'd do something to the car."

"Like what, breathe on it?"

"Like jump on the hood and dent it. Like key the door just for kicks," Jim replied forcefully.

Jenna said nothing, but she knew Jim was right; that's exactly what they would have done. She clicked her lips in disgust, but she decided that it was good Jim was cautious to balance out her wildness.

She also decided she was going to sleep with him.

September 10

Fifteen minutes late counted as on-time in Marlene's world. Judging by her countenance, Missy's teacher would have a firm moral disagreement with that, no doubt red-flagging Marlene as insufficiently engaged in her daughter's education. Marlene apologized profusely. The teacher smiled mechanically. She had the jaw line of a man.

This meeting was to discuss certain issues regarding Missy's behavior. Missy had developed a policy of silent resistance wherein instructions or imperatives were defied without the slightest acknowledgment of authority. She could be told to take a seat; she would ignore the order. She would then be directly confronted, but she would continue to turn a deaf ear. Raised voices made no difference. Gentle physical persuasion only elicited a sharp "No!" and a violent slap at the persuader. Forcibly moving her to her seat would initiate outright screaming followed by an extended bout of violent stares and more silence.

Marlene would have shortened this exposition to "Missy is throwing tantrums," but she was aware how an officious pseudo-clinical tone was the equivalent of High Victorian English in the public school system. She counted herself fortunate that she was spared the suggestion of some vaguely defined syndrome or disorder. Her good fortune didn't hold.

"Does Melissa exhibit similar behavior in the home?"

"Well, no," Marlene replied genially. "She—"

"Even when you ask her to do her reading?"

"No. She loves reading, don't you sweetie?"

Missy nodded apprehensively.

"May I ask about her father?

"Why?"

"I'm trying to get a feeling for the environment at home. Does she get enough attention?"

"She gets my full attention."

"Then perhaps she gets too much attention?"

"Melissa is very well behaved in the home."

"Sometimes problems in the home manifest themselves when the child is away."

Marlene breathed deliberately. "Is there someplace Melissa can go and play while we talk?"

The teacher instructed Missy to go into an adjoining room. Missy did so, wordlessly.

"Isn't it possible," Marlene asked as non-confrontationally as possible, "that since the behavioral problems are occurring at school, that we should investigate the likelihood that this is where the problem may be?"

"Please. I'm really not trying to put you on the defensive."

"I'm not on the defensive. I'm just suggesting—"

"Often, in my experience, children may act out at school in reaction to the home environment. Often this is a question of attention. You're very busy, all single mothers are. Missy may be reacting to the need for more attention—"

Marlene could see that this inane diagnosis was going to have a lasting and possibly irreversible affect on her daughter's life, and her own, and that it was made the minute she showed up late as a single mom, or perhaps even before that.

She decided to resist. "She gets attention at home. A good deal more attention than—" Marlene was about to add, "I got at my age," but she didn't think she could handle the vapidly inevitable "things are different now" response. The alternative "the other children in her class do," would have elicited a condescending "the other children aren't having this problem." She decided to leave it unfinished, but added, "My daughter is the center of my life twenty-four hours a day."

"I think we should try to be constructive about this, we're both here for Melissa's good."

"I'm a little baby! I'm three going on four!" Melissa announced from the doorway of the adjoining room. "Wah! I'm a little baby! I'm three going on four! Wah! I'm three going on four! Wah! I'm three going on four!"

Melissa continued the chant, laughing as she kept at it despite the gentle, rational admonitions of the teacher.

Finally, Marlene snapped, "Stop it! Now!" Melissa quieted and returned to the play room.

Marlene couldn't help but smile. The teacher was not amused. She glared at Marlene and asked, "Have you ever had Melissa checked for ADD?"

Marlene's smile turned to a wince. "She doesn't have ADD."

"But you're not really qualified to make that evaluation, are you?"

Hopeless. It was hopeless. Marlene collected Melissa and resigned herself to having to somehow find a doctor, get the time away from work, and take Melissa to be tested for ADD.

From her car seat in back Missy was repeating the word "no" to some internal rhythm.

Marlene was seething at the thought of everything she wanted to say and everything she should have said to the teacher, then seething deeper when she realized anything she said would have just reinforced the teacher's prejudice.

"No. No. No. Mommy can we get ice cream?"

"No."

"Why not?"

"Because we are going to have dinner soon."

"No. No. No..."

What bullshit anyway! Missy doesn't have ADD, she's six years old. Is she supposed to behave like a charm school debutant?

"I want ice cream!"

"No."

"No. No. No..."

Oh, but I'm not qualified to determine that. She, however, is qualified to jerk me around because she probably read some fucking pamphlet! Bitch!

"Ice cream!"

"Stop it!"

"I'm a little baby! Wah! I'm three going on four..."

Marlene's cell phone went off. "Hello..."

"Mommy!"

"No, I hadn't heard that...can't it be...two-thirty is going to be too..."

"Mommy!"

"...soon, Chad. I know..."

"I'm three going on four. Wah! I'm three going on four..."

"...just a second. Melissa- NO!"

"No. No. No..."

"Ok, I may be a little late...Chad...Chad, can you set up an appointm...well then just email me so I remem..."

"No. No. No..."

"I'm driving, how am I supposed to write it down? Never mind...never mind...yes, ok, good-bye."

"No. No. No..."

"Melissa, please stop that." Marlene was pleading now. Her fingers went into spasm around the steering wheel.

"I want ice cream! Mommy! I want ice cream!"

Marlene pulled off the road and dropped her head into her hands.

"Mommy, why are we stopping? Mommy! Why are

we stopping?"

....

This time the hot Philippina-looking girl took the treadmill next to him. Well, well, well. How to play this? Gotta get inside her head.

She gave an extremely neutral nod of acknowledgement, providing Billy little help.

There were plenty of open treadmills, so it couldn't have been completely unintentional. That would suggest at the very worst there were other people she wanted to tread next to even less than him.

Next question: How does she think she left it last time? Does she even realize she left him feeling like a dirty old man, and a failed one at that, or does she think she smoothly extricated herself leaving him appropriately intrigued at her mysterious femininity? Or maybe it was all part of a Machiavellian plan to perplex him and twist him unknowingly to her will—which, upon further reflection, might be just fine.

Forget it. Keep the goal in mind. Start with the goal and the tactics follow. There were two possible paths. He could, a) go back in hot pursuit as if he were never dissed to begin with, or b) maintain an aloof distance to show he was not some desperate drooler who would put up with her games.

Option (a) would cover him whether she was being apologetic or simply inquisitive. The risk was that it had all been a big shit-test, that she was being inquisitive as to how easily he would come back from regular and rigorous ball-busting sessions in the future, should it come to that. Bad precedent.

Option (b) would make it clear that his balls were unbustable, but it was a possible dead-end in any circumstance where the fragility of his genitals was not the primary question.

The issue was readily resolved when Billy tripped on his own shoelace and was propelled backwards off the end of the treadmill like a stumbling wino.

"Are you all right?" she asked sympathetically.

"Yeah, I'm fine. I meant to do that, actually. It's called power stumbling, really kicks up your heart rate. Graceful exits are for wimps."

She gave a giggle that may or may not have been genuine. "I'll have to try that, do they offer instruction for beginners?"

"I could teach you. Just give me a second to tie your shoelaces together."

She smiled warmly. Now was the time to ask; even if she wanted to get away she couldn't.

"You know, I'd like to talk to you some time when neither of us is out of breath. Do you—?"

Her treadmill program kicked into high gear and he was drowned out by the whining motor and pounding cadence of her strides. He smiled a resigned smile to hide his disappointment, nodded in deference to her workout, and started away knowing another bout of self-pity was in his future.

Then, behind him, he heard the treadmill slow to a crawl. He turned to see her exiting gracefully. "I'm sorry. That was very rude of me. What were you saying?"

They agreed to meet for "a quick drink" at nine that evening. Billy smiled invitingly, hoping she wouldn't notice the sharpness of his teeth.

Back at his apartment, Billy was going through his date prep ritual. Mindlessly rote. He could do it in his sleep. Nearly his entire wardrobe could be labeled quality casual. These were clothes that would fit perfectly at work, where ties had been eschewed years back, but jeans and sweatshirts would be frowned upon. These also worked perfectly on a date, where formality was a sign of unaccustomed insecurity and slovenliness a sign of a loser.

As Billy dressed he simultaneously set out a bunch of stuff to take with him back to Marlene's afterwards, including some toiletries that would cause Missy to giggle at him for smelling like a girl and Marlene to murmur in lascivious approval. He caught himself before applying some—no point raising questions when he returned to Marlene's.

A quick double check in the mirror: Black cap toes, gray cotton-linen flat-fronts, and a black pullover with subtle touches of stimulating red. At the door he stopped to consider taking his laptop along with the other stuff. He was pretty sure there was nothing incriminating on it and besides, it was password protected. Missy would enjoy playing video games with him. But can you ever be sure? And what if Marlene asked for his password as some test of intimacy? He wasn't anywhere near ready to provide anyone full access to his email archives and personal calendar, or worse, his browser history. Better leave it. He dialed Marlene.

"Hello," she sighed.

"Whoa. You've had a bad day."

"Frustrating. I met with Missy's teacher today. I could use a drink."

Billy cringed. "Sounds good to me. Look, I'm going to be late. I'm gonna grab a quick drink with a friend and then I'm going to stop by my place and get some more stuff."

"Oh."

"When I get there, I will personally pour you a drink and give you a back rub."

"Well, are you going to eat out?"

"Yeah, I'll probably have something disgusting at the bar."

"OK, then."

"Is everything OK?" Billy asked as sympathetically as possible.

"Yeah, it's fine. I'll see you whenever you get here."

"OK, bye."

"Bye."

Chilly, very chilly. But a bottle of chocolate liqueur should be enough to set things right.

••••

It was dark, and even though it was not cold Sarah felt a chill through her tissue-lean skin. Yoga did that to her, as if she were stretched membrane-thin so that even the absence of light could cool her. She walked past the noisy hullabaloo of shops and restaurants, mindful of her flow, her gait, her spiritual center. Tonight she should record some contemplative thoughts in her journal but, shamefully, she knew she would probably watch a reality show or some other soulless activity. Passing Ben & Jerry's she chose the lesser defilement of chocolate mint ice cream, and forcibly dismissed the notion that her choice was made to avoid the detached solitude of her apartment.

Size small, please. In a cup, not a cone.

The cold would be good for her. It would equalize her internal body temperature with her skin. Letting the ice cream slowly melt before removing the plastic spoon from her mouth, she inattentively flipped through whatever random tabloid or newspaper section had been left by previous patrons.

Out the front window she saw Billy pause next to some restaurant. Whether she liked or disliked the sight of him she could not decide and knew she shouldn't try. She hoped he wouldn't see her looking all pathetic eating ice cream by herself, even though she wasn't pathetic, she was just having some ice cream, like millions of people do everyday and besides if she were really pathetic she would be hiding from him, which she wasn't.

Within a few seconds, as if it were planned, a young, provocatively dressed Asian woman met him. They had a brief exchange and entered the restaurant. Sarah quickly finished her small cup of chocolate mint ice cream.

••••

Guidelines for meeting a woman for a quick drink, amalgamated from any number of glossy lad mags:

Timing—odds are she will arrive late. This is a power play. It implies she is sacrificing her important time for you so you owe her. DO NOT let this succeed. Of course, you don't want to out-late her because there is nothing that will shut a woman down faster than waiting alone in a bar. The best play is to position yourself so that you can see the entrance and "arrive" immediately after she does. This will foil the lateness game, often to her obvious disappointment. If there is no such opportunity, arrive just late enough that it can be passed off as a rounding error, then wait no more than ten minutes at which point send a text message such as "Sorry you couldn't make it. Best of luck with whatever came up." If she replies immediately, you now have the upper hand. Otherwise, move on.

Demonstrate subtle dominance. Ask what she wants, then order for both of you. Have a change of venue in mind and suggest it forthrightly, just to be the guide of events. At one point subvert the conversation to a topic of interest to you and show some passion about it (but only once, don't overdo this). Always order the more manly drink. If she orders white wine, you order red. If she orders red, you order scotch. If she orders scotch, make yours a double.

Engage her mind not through reason, but subtle confusion and intrigue. Generally speaking, no more than three outright compliments should be offered and these should be oblique and non-obvious. Do not tell a beautiful woman she is beautiful. Never tell a smart-mouthed cutie that you admire her attitude.   Never tell a social activist that you are impressed with her conviction. Never tell a double-D she has a great rack. The best compliments are unexpected and indirect, leaving her wondering if it was really intended as a compliment. For a woman, this counts as intellectual stimulation.

If food is involved, order what you please. You have appetites. She needs to see and appreciate that.

At some level, consciously or not, she has the intent to attract you physically, so at the end of preliminaries do not be shy about acting on your attraction; whatever the situation calls for, from a tender kiss or a full-on grope, despite her reaction, it is not unexpected. Always Be Closing.

There were lots of rules. None of this took much effort anymore. Billy kept a mental database of a few places that were perfect for "observing the entrance" or "a change of venue". If there was one thing Billy had down pat, it was dating.

••••

She was showing too much skin for a "quick date", Billy astutely observed, then quickly castigated himself for even entertaining the concept of "too much skin." She approached and acknowledged Billy with a friendly smile, then even before the exchange of greetings she looked at his shoes. Billy immediately knew what he was in for. From years of reading women's magazines, and possibly occasional forays into the lad mags of her boyfriends (which she would find much more interesting), she had obviously developed a litany of

Things To Look For On A First Date. Old hat to Billy.

Shoes. Is he wearing sneakers? A sure sign of continuing adolescence—run away! Big, solid Doc Martens? He hasn't purchased shoes since the mid-'90s—sorry, pass. Clogs? That's just wrong—next, please. Look for nicely maintained classic styles in brown or black. (Boat shoes are an immediate disqualification in the evening. In the daylight, simply a warning sign.)

Old hat to the point of being wearying.

The improbably named Midge let Billy know that she really only had time for one drink. Of course, she did.

Create an escape hatch early on. You don't have to use it, but if you need it, you'll be grateful.

Billy held the door for her and told the hostess they were just going to sit at the bar if that's OK. He guided her to one of the tall cocktail tables by applying nearly imperceptible pressure to the small of her back, helped her off with her coat, and took the chair next to her. He asked her what she would like and when she said white wine he quickly glanced at the stand-up wine list on the table and ordered a Pinot Grigio and a Merlot, even though he would have sacrificed a non-critical internal organ for a double scotch on the rocks at that moment. He stopped the waitress and changed the Merlot to a single malt.

Is he confident, but not boastful? Does he disregard and dictate or does he act decisively on your lead?

"I'm glad we finally get to talk when we're not drenched in sweat and hyperventilating. Have you always been very athletic?"

This, Billy knew, was the perfect thing to say. It was the only experience they really had in common and it was also complimentary to her in an unexpected way. She was strikingly beautiful and had probably been told that on every date of her life, but rarely would a man have complimented her athletic ability.

"Oh, well I've never really done any sports. I was a dancer, though. I mean I was on the dance squad in high school."

"That must have been fun. What kind of dance...?"

And they were off; from high school, to how did she decide to go to college here, to plans for after graduate school, to where she would choose to live afterwards, to places she'd traveled to or would like to see.

Billy used the topic of travel to switch the focus to himself.

> *Does he constantly talk about himself? If so, limit your suffering by employing your escape hatch as soon as possible. His focus should be on you since you are the reason he's there. But: beware the man who reveals nothing. At best, it shows fear of intimacy; at worst, he's married.*

Despite the tiresome date-speak interplay, the conversation flowed smoothly and Billy's fatigue slipped away. By ten o'clock, they were half way through their second round, and under that influence, Midge loosened up a bit and became talkative—almost bubbly. She went on about the "p-chem" research she was doing which went straight over Billy's head, but he admired her enthusiasm. She was actually a terrific girl. She had a dark, exotic beauty. She gave him some friendly ribbing about his first hand knowledge of those old TV shows and at one point replied, "An Audi. Wow. I bet chicks really dig you now," showing a bit of attitude. Billy liked her and that replenished his energy. His weariness gone, thoughts of closing began to form.

As she finished up her second glass of wine, she excused herself to go to "the powder room." The waitress approached while she was gone and Billy considered ordering another round, to some extent because he was fairly certain he could get her in bed, but before he could order the waitress handed him a folded piece of paper and said, "From the lady at the end of the bar."

Billy looked over and saw no one.

"Well, she was there a minute ago," the waitress offered with a shrug, and left.

Billy opened the piece of paper and written on it

in large, blood-red, block letters was: YOU ARE A
LYING CHEATING PIECE OF SHIT. He scanned and
scrutinized everyone he could see, but there was no
one he recognized nor did anyone avert their eyes or
give any other indication of guilt.

When Midge returned he forced a smile and said,
"I'm so glad you came out tonight. I had a good
time."

"Oh, uh, yes, it was very nice," she replied reflexively,
obviously not expecting that the evening was over.

"Time passed so quickly," said Billy. "Our one quick
drink was turning into a late night."

Billy was probably violating a number of first date
precepts and under normal circumstances would
have suggested they go somewhere to grab a
snack or maybe some old sitcoms on his plasma,
but the all-too-accurate accusation of shithood had
thoroughly disrupted his game.

She talked nervously until they reached her car
when she asked, "You think I'm a stupid kid, don't
you?"

"What? No."

"I was nervous, because I like you and all, but I've never been out with anyone your age."

Billy smiled incredulously.

"I'm sorry," she said.

"Are you kidding? You were great."

"Really?"

"Yes. You're beautiful and fun. What's not to like? Does it bother you that I'm older than you?"

"No, I just..."

"Look, you're a terrific girl. I just hadn't really planned on a late night, you know. You seemed pretty tentative about things to begin with."

"I know. I was just nervous."

"I know."

There was a pause. Midge reached for her keys and opened her door. Billy wanted to kiss her. He didn't. What he did was say, "I'll give you a call," which was exactly the wrong thing to do. He could have kissed her and said maybe we'll meet again; that would have been correct. He would have gotten a kiss—a minor erotic moment—and not necessarily been on the hook to call her. But no, he managed to get himself the reverse. He choked and he knew it. Little crossed his mind on the drive home save blind profanity.

••••

"Mommy, do boobs give you power?"

"What?"

"Do boobs give you power?"

"Sweetie, I don't understand what you mean."

"On TV. They said strip dancers show their boobs because it gives them power."

"Lovely."

Missy was painstakingly drawing a picture of a house and didn't seem too intent on getting a straight answer, which was good because Marlene didn't have one. In fact, she was fairly certain an appropriate answer did not exist. She had long ago accepted that monitoring television was something she would have had to make a career of. For all she knew, "strip dancers" could have been a topic of discussion on Tori Tornado.

"Mommy, is it better to have big boobs or little boobs?"

"It doesn't make any difference, Missy."

"You have little boobs."

"I have average boobs."

"Jenna has big boobs."

"Jenna's shirts are too tight."

"Do you think I will have big boobs or little boobs?"

"I don't know, honey. Which do you want?"

"Big ones. Until I'm older and then little ones."

Marlene laughed involuntarily. "Why?"

"Big boobs to start so I have more power, but if you have little boobs they don't sag so much after nursing."

"Good Lord, Melissa! Where did you hear that?"

"Pammy. She said she wished her boobs were smaller so they wouldn't be so saggy from nursing her boys. Then she said she wanted to get a boob job to fix them. Mommy, what's a boob job?"

"When did she say that?"

"In the hot tub."

Hence the futility of monitoring TV. Throughout the entire conversation Missy had not looked up from her drawing. Her queries were made from the purest of innocence, while Marlene could only listen in the purest of horror.

The phone chirped. Checking the caller ID, Marlene answered with, "So, you wish your boobs were less saggy and you're thinking of getting a boob job."

"Did I get the psychic hotline by mistake?"

"That's what my daughter told me."

"Your daughter told you?"

Marlene laughed. "We've been having a very serious conversation about boobs. Frightening. She overheard you say that in the hot tub."

"Oh God! You don't think she repeated that at school, do you?"

"I don't know. If you start getting calls from all the plastic surgeons in the school district, then we'll know for sure."

"Great. Listen, is Flip over there hanging out with Billy?"

"Nope. Billy isn't home yet." Marlene wasn't sure whether 'home' was the right word.

"Oh," replied Pammy, unsure whether that was a casual comment or a bit of bitterness that needed validation. She decided on the later. "So he hasn't moved in completely yet?"

"Is that a shock?" replied Marlene confirming Pammy's decision.

"At least you're getting sex out of the deal. I have all Flip's stuff in my house and get no sex whatsoever. I think you've got the better deal."

"Well…"

"You mean you're not getting any either?"

"Let's just say I'm not getting anything to write home about."

"Ah ha. Limp will, limp dick."

Marlene was usually repelled by Pammy's casual explicitness, but she had to be impressed with how she summed up what would be weeks of couples therapy in one terse phrase.

"Where the hell is Flip? You know he was down in the basement working on—Stop that! What are you doing? Put that down! No! No! You cannot cut your brother's hair with a steak knife! Put it down! Put! It! Down! Tell you what, I'll come over and talk boobs with Missy if you come over here and ping-pong my boys around for a while."

Marlene noted how Pammy liberally employed the possessive. Her house, her boys. "Ha!"

"He's not in the house, but the car is here."

"Maybe he ran away from home," Marlene suggested casually.

"No, he would have taken the beer from the fridge. Besides it's not like I asked him to have sex with me, I just asked him to replace the toilet seats."

"If I see him I'll send him straight home."

"Thanks, Mar. Bye."

"Bye."

Pammy hung up wondering whether the problem was with Billy or that Marlene was a prissy little ice-princess.

Marlene hung up speculating that if she were living in *her* home with *her* boys, she might go AWOL too. Then she wondered how much of their conversation Missy might have intuited from the one side she heard.

••••

Flip leered out across his lawn and down the street. His eyes fixed on Marlene's silhouette behind the shade as she talked on the phone. It was obvious from the outline that her figure hadn't settled in her lower half, like the goddam ball-and-chain. It occurred to him that she might undress right then and there so he instinctively slipped back into the shadows where he almost broke his ankle tripping over a child's bicycle.

"Goddam it!" he announced to the night sky. "The next time I find a goddam bike on the goddam lawn I'm gonna throw it out with the goddam trash!" Not personal enough, he thought. "Along with the nearest goddam brat I can find!"

His bellows only registered on the walls of the houses up and down the block. He glanced back up at Marlene but she had moved out of sight.

Just then, Otto's non-descript domestic sedan rolled out of the garage again and lurched down the street. Flip reached for the child's bike, tempted to hurl it through his windshield as he passed. Instead he drew himself up to full, ex-high school linebacker height, folded his arms defiantly and cast the most menacing glare he could as Otto rolled by. Otto didn't notice. He just drove on past the little island that so desperately needed a fountain and on out into the world. Flip sneered. Probably going out in search of some shady deal for junk that he'll sell on eBay and make a goddam fortune. That, and a tall stack at IHOP.

Flip looked back and considered Otto's darkened house for a long moment then dissolved into the shadows again.

••••

Jenna thought she should cry, but she didn't feel like

crying. She felt more like eating, but she was not about to suggest she and Jim go over to Wendy's as if life would just go on like it always had. Judging from her reflection in the visor vanity mirror she didn't look particularly happy or sad, just normal, except she could have used a hair brush.

Jim didn't look particularly happy either. If anything he looked apologetic. He awkwardly slipped his hand behind her neck and she contorted to reach across the center console and gear shift to complete the hug. So strange. Is that how you know when sex ends, when it's just too uncomfortable to go on? As Jim exited the car briefly to dispose of the condom, her thoughts were not about her lost virginity, but Jim's littering.

Virginity lost, yet she was unchanged and disturbingly unemotional. She felt compelled to tell people. Like the girls in school; the ones who claimed to have done it. She stepped through the litany of her friends and their supposed sexual status, trying to use her new experience to gauge who was lying and who wasn't.

Maybe they could tell by looking at her. She stole another look in the visor mirror but it was still just her. What if her parents could tell? Gawd! Her father would hide his shock on principle and then start lecturing her about responsibility and safe-sex. Her mom would smile weakly and start to cry pathetically and wonder if it was her fault and if she did something wrong. Gawd! Jenna winced in virtual embarrassment.

At that moment Jenna hated everything. All the phoniness and mendacity. All the egocentrics who would belittle her love—yes, Love!—for Jim and behave as if it only affected them. All the closed-minded wisdom. There had to be a better way to live than this! She just hated this stupid place!

"I hate this," said Jimbo quietly. "I hate sneaking around. I hate this car. I want to be in bed with you. It would have been much better. I promise." He seemed close to tears, still looking apologetic.

Now, at last, Jenna burst into tears, convinced that she had changed so much; obviously and irrevocably. But she was still surrounded by the fools of her forgone youth. She wanted to explode in anger. She wanted to vanish in sorrow. "I need a hair brush," she sobbed.

In a whisper, Jimbo just kept saying, "I'm sorry."

••••

Billy wheeled his Audi slowly through the neighborhood, mindful to keep below the 25 mph speed limit because, like the sign said: Treasured Children Playing. Also, he didn't want to receive an amended note accusing him of being a LYING CHEATING *SPEEDING* PIECE OF SHIT.

The blinding brightness of the neighborhood had condensed into thick shafts of yellow radiating from windows where curtains happened to be undrawn. Billy lifted off the accelerator and glided smoothly into Marlene's driveway. He doused the headlights and locked the doors manually so the beeping report of the key fob would not cause someone to emerge from a nearby home and label him a LYING CHEATING SPEEDING *BEEPING* PIECE OF SHIT.

Be logical. Did it have to be someone who knew him and Marlene and the current situation, or could it have been a practical joke that happened to be a little more poignant than intended? If whoever it was knew Marlene, why not just tell Marlene? Maybe as a warning? Maybe to not ruin things, but compel him to behave? One of the windows radiating light was Marlene's bedroom. Billy looked up at it.

Well, fuck whoever it was! What business was that of anyone's? Besides, did he not have plausible deniability here? He had told Marlene he was meeting a friend for a drink, and that's exactly what he did, right? Fuck it.

Turning away from the window and scanning the neighborhood, he could just make out Otto milling about in shrubbery beside his house and the end of the street. That presented an opportunity. He could approach him with a disarming "Otto? Is that you? I thought someone suspicious might be lurking about." Combine that with the fact that Billy was the only one who didn't treat him like an infectious leper and maybe he could convince Otto to part with a Tori Tornado doll for Missy.

It was a very eerie experience, walking down a suburban street at night. There was a wilderness level silence that awakened a primal adrenaline rush. You never got this silence in the city; no rumbling cars, no dopplering sirens, no indistinct nearby conversations. Random shafts of lights up and down the streets were like the distant fires of unfamiliar settlements. They could represent opportunity or danger—friends or foes. What did he know of the people behind them? Were they looking and judging, ready to fire off anonymous accusations of shithood? Or were they ready to offer communal acceptance—provided there was a need he could fulfill, perhaps? For that matter, what did he really know of anyone at all in this world, beyond a tiny glimpse through their reactions to him? Even Marlene. Hell, what did anyone really know of anyone? Doubt is fear. No wonder places like this inspired hockey-masked, machete-wielding incarnations of pure evil.

As he drew close, he could see that it wasn't Otto after all. Nor was it someone suspicious. It was Flip; hands cupped around his eyes, trying to see into Otto's basement window.

Billy quietly walked up from behind and said, "Busted."

Flip emitted a short, wide-eyed scream and spun around off balance, falling into the shrubbery as he attempted to swear at Billy in response.

Billy laughed.

"Shut up!" Flip hissed. A few more choice words were whispered in anger as he struggled to extract himself from the bushes.

"You lose a golf ball or something?"

"No, smart guy, I didn't lose a golf ball," Flip snapped turning back to the basement window. "I just know that bastard is hoarding Tori Tornado dolls in there. I wanted to see it with my own eyes."

"Are you serious?"

"Hell yes I'm serious."

"So what are you gonna do if he's got 'em, break in and steal them?"

Flip said nothing for a moment, then, "Why not?"

"How about because you'll get caught, go to prison, and spend your days modeling lingerie for a 400-lb. lifer with a missing ear and a tattoo of his pit bull."

"I won't get caught. I just got to plan it out right. Besides stealing a Tori Tornado doll would be a misdemeanor. That's jail, not prison. Hell, I'm a solid family man. I'll probably get off with community service."

"Well, when you put it like that, it makes perfect sense."

"It does. Why should that fat prick get all the dolls? Do you think that's right? Don't you think we all should have an equal chance?"

"Sure, you're just demanding your constitutional right to equal access to Tori Tornado. What do you want a doll for anyway? You have three boys."

"Maybe I'll sell it and get back the money to cover what it cost me to arrange for that fountain. Plus, replace the garbage can he dented."

"Like I said, makes perfect sense." Silently, Billy vowed that if Flip did get away with it, he'd buy the doll from him to give to Missy. In fact, it was entirely possible that his best interest would be served by encouraging Flip. "How many dolls do you see in there?" Billy asked.

"I can't see anything; it's too dark." Flip squatted down even closer to the window and squinted intently. Billy joined him, as if two sets of eyes might be able to make something out.

"What are you guys doing?" Dick asked.

A substantial number of f-bombs were dropped in the ensuing thirty seconds it took Flip and Billy to remove themselves from the shrubbery.

"Well," whispered Billy, "Flip is planning the heroic liberation of one or more Tori Tornados from the enemy's basement prison camp."

Dick's eyes widened. "He's got those dolls in there? I knew it. Greedy bastard."

Dick squatted down to join Flip peering into the opaque basement.

"You have got to be kidding me," said Billy.

"Hey—either help us, or be quiet," Flip suggested.

"Yeah," agreed Dick. "So do you see anything in there?"

"Maybe. Over to the far left, there some kind of shape—" Flip replied.

"I can't see it."

"Way in back. See that thing that looks like a pile of rags? I think that's it."

"Oh yeah, I see it. Kind of."

"God knows it couldn't actually be a pile of rags. Who would have something like that in the corner of their basement?" offered Billy.

Headlight beams flashed across the night. "Car!" whispered Flip and they all crouched in the shadows. It was Jimbo dropping off Jenna. The three watched from hiding as Jenna emerged from the passenger side, her exposed midriff noticeably more luminous than the other colors in the scene. Jimbo met her as she came past the hood, his hands in his pocket, and walked her to the door. They hugged for a moment too long and in a pose too intimate to simply be a casual good-bye. They kissed innocently enough. Then she entered the house and Jimbo walked back to the car, hands in pockets.

The significance of the body language was not lost on Billy, who was pretty sure they had just had sex. Flip and Dick were too pre-occupied with Tori Tornado to notice.

As attention returned to the basement window, Billy suggested that before they go any further they should start using false names. He would be Mr. Black.

"Um, alright, I'll be Mr. Jones, I guess," Dick offered, oblivious.

Billy sighed in exasperation. "How about you, Flip?"

"Fuck you," Flip offered.

"Flip, you can't possibly see anything. C'mon, let's go before he gets back."

"Oh, I've seen enough," Flip replied, rising to his feet and brushing himself off. "Just one more thing."

Flip darted around behind Otto's house. Dick and Billy exchanged looks of apprehension. In a moment, they saw a dim image of two metal garbage cans following a parabolic trajectory into the air and landing in the middle of Otto's back yard.

Flip reappeared, giggling. "OK, now we can go."

"You're out of your mind," theorized Billy as they turned to beat a hasty retreat.

"Hey, what's going on?"

The trio tried to stop short but their legs slipped out from under them and they landed in unison on their backsides.

"Dammit, Jimbo!" exclaimed Flip.

"Hi, Jim. What are you doing here?" asked Dick in his best I'm-friendly-with-my-daughter's-boyfriend tone.

"I was just dropping off Jenna and I saw you guys—"

"Did you have a nice date?"

"Yeah, you know. The usual. So what are you all doing?"

"Just gathering a little intel," Flip said slyly.

Billy elaborated. "Flip was doing some reconnaissance for potential felony breaking and entering…"

"It's not a felony," Flip interrupted.

"…and topped it off with a bit of misdemeanor vandalism, just for kicks." In the distance, Billy spotted Jenna walking over to Marlene's. Could Jenna have written that note? "Dick and I were trying to work out false names for everyone. You're welcome to join the gang, but you'll have to be Mr. Pink."

"Forget it, then," Jimbo deadpanned.

"Alright, alright," Dick intoned. "We need to split up

so we aren't seen together."

"Good idea," replied Billy. "Um, why?"

Dick looked at Billy like he was retarded. "Because if we are seen together it will look like we are up to something."

"Well, my car is off to the left, so I'll go off of the left," Jimbo graciously offered.

"Ok, then. Billy, you cross the street and head up the opposite side. I'll cut through the back yards over there. Flip you go the long way around the block to the right."

"What is going on down there?" a voice screeched from far off. It was Pammy, in a bathrobe, shouting from the street in front of her house. "Flip, what are you doing? Get back home!"

"Sorry, Hon! Be right there!"

"OK, new plan," said Billy. "Flip you go straight home."

Flip went straight home, muttering under his breath.

"Later guys," Jimbo said, casually walking to his car.

"OK, we'll meet up later to finalize our plans," Dick whispered.

"What? You're not serious about this, are you?" Billy reasoned. "Flip is insane, you know."

"This needs to be done. It's a blow for fairness and justice in our community. I don't know about you, but I don't give in to fascism."

Dick shuffled off to make his furtive escape through his neighbor's back yards.

Billy glanced around the once again quiet suburban street. There were fewer lights on now and one could just barely make out a couple of lonely stars overhead. A gentle cool breeze stood in contrast to the oppressive heat of the day. He shook his head and trod back to Marlene's.

As he was unlocking the door, he paused to watch Otto's car slithering through the neighborhood and into his garage.

Billy had no idea what to make of any of this.

••••

Jenna was wearing a deep aqua t-shirt with the words *Pool Party* in script across the chest. Billy looked away hoping Jimbo was appreciative of such things.

Jenna and Marlene were engaged in an intense confab. Although Billy was deeply apprehensive about the possible topic, he said nothing out of the ordinary.

"You didn't have to baby-sit tonight, did you Jenna?" he asked, furrowing his brow in confusion.

Jenna smiled but didn't answer.

Marlene said, "No, we're just chatting," and gave Billy a forceful roll of the eyes indicating that he should go away.

"Well, I think I'll go check on Missy," said Billy on his way up the stairs. He paused at the top to briefly eavesdrop.

"Did you use a condom?" Marlene asked once they were alone.

Billy said a short prayer of thanks before finishing

his climb.

"Well, not at first, but then we did. But I don't think it matters. I don't think he, you know...finished. It was so uncomfortable in that stupid little car."

"Honey, you need to be careful..."

Jenna started to cry, "Please don't tell my Mom."

"OK, honey, but, you know, it's probably OK if you tell her. She'll understand."

"No she won't. She won't handle it. She'll get all weird and weepy and I can't take that."

"Honey, believe it or not, your Mom has had sex. At least once."

"No, I was left by aliens. It was a reverse abduction." Jenna laughed at herself through her tears. "I can't even talk to my Mom about buying a bra, never mind sex."

Marlene vowed she would never let things get like this between her and Missy. She silently prayed to God to take her before Missy had sex.

"My Mom doesn't know what to say, so she starts crying and says something about how it breaks her heart to see me growing up. Gawd! Please don't tell her."

"I won't. I won't. Don't worry about it." Marlene knew she was probably breaking the unspoken code of motherhood, but telling wouldn't make Jenna talk to her Mom and it would prevent Jenna from ever confiding in her again, leaving the poor girl with no adult to talk to.

"Do you think he'll say anything to anyone?" Jenna wondered.

"You mean like brag to his friends? I don't know. He doesn't seem like the type."

"He's withdrawn, you mean?"

"Maybe not withdrawn…"

"Quiet? Shy?"

"Well behaved." Marlene realized instantly that that made him sound dull. "I mean in the sense of being mature."

"I'm wild though, aren't I? Am I too wild? Is he going to think I'm too wild for him now?"

"I don't think so, honey. He probably likes that about you."

"You mean because he might just be with me because I'm wild enough to have sex with him?"

"No, honey, I mean I'm sure he cares about you a lot."

"You think so? I hope so, because I'm in love with him and I'm glad I waited...for...someone...I..." Jenna's choked sobs prevented her from finishing. Suddenly her mood changed from sentiment to frustration. "I can't wait to get out of this place. I hate it here."

Marlene went into listen-only mode. Jenna was living in a swirl of emotional and delusional bedlam, unsusceptible to reason.

••••

"Missy is asking for her mom to tuck her in," said Billy in a low, careful voice. "Is everything OK with Jenna?"

"Yes, just a teenage crisis."

Still without an accurate read, Billy walked up behind Marlene and slipped a hand around her waist. She languidly shifted her weight into his chest to his consummate relief. It was not the body language due a cheating, lying piece of shit. Marlene angled her head back and offered her neck for his pleasure. He instinctively obliged, but eased himself free in a moment and casually pulled a bottle of water from the refrigerator. Without reaction, she stepped over to the trash bin and lifted and tied the mostly full bag from it.

"I'll be right back," she announced without feeling.

Billy cursed himself. This was a new low. He should have taken her right there—just pulled her slacks down and bent her over the kitchen table. Wimp. Eunuch.

····

From the garage window, Marlene saw Jenna disappear into her house. She pulled a teal blue scarf out of a corner nook and wrapped her head, then soundlessly removed all of her clothing, carefully hanging her blouse to cover the tiny window to the back yard. In the opposite corner, she reached to rusted coffee can on a high shelf and retrieved half a pack of Winston cigarettes and a purple Bic lighter. Taking a moment to wedge as much of her hair up under the scarf as possible, she lit a cigarette, and puffed rapidly while thinking, "Damn."

After every couple of puffs she would go open the side door and oscillate it a few times to purge the excess smoke, hoping the batches were small enough not to be noticed by the neighbors. The breeze on her bare skin prompted her to fantasize about simply walking out to the cul-de-sac island and spending a few minutes languorously puffing away in the nude. She might have even skinny dipped in the fountain if there were one. The cold of the cement floor on her feet caused her to stand on one foot, alternately. She started to puff double time. Years ago, in a college art history elective they had discussed the difference between naked and nude. At that moment she was definitely naked. "Damn," she said aloud and started puffing triple time.

She snuffed out the cigarette and pushed it to the very bottom of the half-full trash can, then waved the smoke out the garage one last time before whipping off the teal blue scarf and re-dressing.

••••

Jimbo knew he was frowning but no amount of will power could relax his brow. The kitchen smelled of white wine. Over the years the smell must have permeated the Formica table top; hell, just about every smell known to man probably infested that table. He recalled throwing up a can of Spaghettios on it in third grade, right in front of little Suzie Faldo who had come over to work on a school project. A year later his babysitter Jilly Sampson—the one with the perfect, moist pout that made him first correlate kissing with that ticklish feeling between his legs— kept yelling at her loutish boyfriend for trying to lay her down on the table, crushing Jimbo's model of a Porsche 911 and squirting airplane glue all over.

"When are you going to have that girlfriend of yours over to meet us?" His mom appeared in her bathrobe, swirling her wine in a plastic tumbler.

Maybe he wasn't any good at sex. Jenna seemed to think it was OK, but girls talk about things. How was she going to describe it to her friends?

Were stunted, snarky, uncapitalized text messages flying through cyberspace to the bulk of the female student body at this moment? "Maybe soon."

She hiccupped slightly and sat down at the table. The flush of the downstairs water closet, followed by the inevitable jigging of the handle heralded his father's entrance. He smiled behind thick framed glasses, snapped the elastic of his boxers and announced, "I feel ten pounds lighter."

His Mom's abdominal folds shuddered slightly in good humor. "Well, I hope it's safe in there."

Jim left. He passed his younger sister sitting on the blue serge couch in front of the TV, chowing down handfuls of broken potato chips with unwarranted alacrity. "I newedoodoo dwy mm do bahn pawacish."

Jimbo ignored her, trod upstairs, humbly washed his genitals, and lay in bed with his palms against the ridges in his forehead. The branch from the large oak outside his windows brushed irregularly against the house. As a child his plans for escape involved making a superhero leap for that branch and swinging to safety and freedom. As recently as a couple of years ago Hank Lockhart, the bully from across the street, was modifying a late model Honda Civic to achieve something called "maximum hoonage." By that time, Hank was too old to bully anyone without opening the possibility of assault and battery charges, so instead of a black eye and a wedgie, Jimbo got a steady stream of commands to engage in various forms of inter-species buggery when he walked over to look on. That didn't prevent his tree descent-fantasy from gaining the theft of a neighbor's hopped-up rice racer, and the (friendly) kidnapping of Jilly Sampson and her pout for the perfect finish.

"Jim!" The shout from downstairs started him out of his reverie. He lay silent.

"Jim! Jim!" He remained silent, disinclined to raise his voice for any reason.

"Jim!" Even louder this time. His mom had boundless reserves of fortitude when it came to hollering across the house, entirely oblivious to the possibility that he might be in the bathroom or otherwise indisposed.

"Jim!"

"What!"

"You need to drive your sister to band practice tomorrow!"

"Fine!" Then adding, "You couldn't climb the stairs and speak like a normal person?" without enough volume to be heard.

Just outside the tree branch was still brushing against the house. He reached for the controller to his soon-to-be-two-generations-old Playstation and occupied his mind in the sickly LCD glow of Grand Theft Auto.

September 15

This naked Tuesday was on a Saturday and it began tentatively since the sun was only technically below the horizon. The brief vestige of dusk at the start was causing everyone to stand around and wait for someone else to make the first move to disrobe. Pammy did so, shortly after making the first move with the champagne.

"Lord knows what they are going to do with them," said Marlene.

"I'm more afraid for the townfolk at large," replied Pammy.

Some concerted arm-twisting had forced the males to take the children out for the evening leaving just enough time for a quick, somewhat ill-timed Naked Tuesday.

"You think Billy will be OK with Missy?" asked Pammy, realizing that Marlene's comment may not have been entirely glib.

"Oh sure. If I'm worried about anything it's that he'll indulge her when he shouldn't. Like take her to Hooter's."

"What!" came a startled cry from the other three.

"Melissa is at the point where she is completely pre-occupied with breasts."

"Flip's that way too."

"How big will mine be? What happens if I let boys see them? When can I get a bra? The other day she asked if we could go to Hooter's for dinner."

"Oh, no."

"I never talked about breasts with Jenna," Dora

chimed in.

There was a brief pause as the others steeled themselves for a bout of weepy remembrance from Dora. Sarah, managed to distract her with a question, "Did Jenna go with them tonight?"

"Oh, heavens no. Jenna wouldn't be caught dead in public with her father. She's been so distant. I'm afraid I'm losing her." No use. The tears began.

"She seems OK to me," offered Marlene.

Sarah and Pammy stared at Marlene, passing the silent message that it was not such a good idea to point out how Jenna was closer to her than her mother. Marlene grimaced in understanding.

"I mean, when she stops by to baby-sit, she seems just like a normal teenage girl."

"Ha. 'Normal' and 'teenage' aren't even on the same planet," pointed out Pammy.

Dora remained on track. "All I want is for her to be happy. Oh I never should have divorced Dick. You always have to put your children first, and I didn't do that. That's what did it, you know. Divorce does that to children, no matter what your reason."

"Adolescence does that to children," Pammy snarked.

Marlene tried to turn the tide, "Dora, honey, look how you've blossomed since your divorce. Don't you think it's good for Jenna to see you like this instead of all unhappy and frustrated?"

"I have?"

"Sure. You're living on your own for the first time in your life. Think about what a good message that sends to Jenna about independence," Marlene said in a firm, get-a-grip tone.

Sarah had a number of comments on living alone that she was careful to suppress, instead suggesting, "Maybe you need an outside interest. You should come to one of my classes, you might find it centering."

"Oh I could never wear spandex. I'm too heavy. I don't know why; I watch what I eat but I can never lose weight."

It took all of Pammy's willpower not to audibly sigh.

Marlene stepped back up to bat. "Honey, why do you let yourself get depressed like that? You know none of us are perfect...oh hell, have a slice of cake."

Tension eased as mouths filled.

"How are things with Billy?" asked Sarah.

"He's not all here yet. If you know what I mean."

"He's a tomcat," Sarah declared coyly.

"He's very good with Missy."

"Everybody seems to have warmed-up to him," offered Dora.

"Isn't he such the charmer?" added Sarah.

"He's just uncomfortable. He's trying," Marlene suggested.

"No doubt," Sarah said.

Marlene regarded Sarah with narrowed eyes.

"Whatever you do, don't marry him. Or at least picture him thirty pounds heavier, in jockeys, with black socks and sandals, one finger up his nose and another in the jar of peanut butter," suggested Pammy.

"Anyone we know?" Marlene laughed.

"Oh my god! That's Dick!" exclaimed Dora.

More cake was consumed.

"Sarah, honey," Marlene intrigued, "We never hear about your love life. Are you seeing anybody?"

"No. Nobody. I'm trying not to. I'm convinced it's possible to be happy without a man."

Pammy smirked, knowing they were being chastised again for only talking about men.

"I should do something," Dora declared as a deeply considered response to a long passed question. "Maybe I should do charity work."

Sarah perked up, "That's a great idea. I know a bunch of programs that are looking for help—environmental watch groups, homeless outreach—"

"You know, Dick mentioned something about new parent-teacher program that gets children involved in the community. It's only volunteer, but I have the time. Of course, it's through the school so Dick will probably want to—"

"Which program is that?" inquired Marlene.

"It's called the Youth Advocate Program. You pick a specific community issue and get the children involved in all aspects of the project, to get them accustomed to societal awareness. They get to see it through from start to finish, all the organizing and planning—"

"How old are the kids?"

"Oh all ages. You know Missy would probably get a kick out of it."

"Well, I'm not sure she would appreciate it—"

"Your boys could do it too. It would get them away from the TV."

"That's not a good idea," replied Pammy. "I think that would technically be community *dis*service. The only time they'll end up doing community service is in lieu of jail time."

"This is good cake where did you buy it?"

"Just up at the grocery store."

"That's what I should do for the boy's birthday. It's not like they'll appreciate it if I make one."

"You know Dick was such a pig at our wedding that he actually fingered the cake before we cut it."

"Flip spent our entire reception trying to get his buddies hooked up with my bridesmaids."

"I used to love being a bridesmaid. I was a bridesmaid four times in one year."

"Nice to have a closet full of ugly dresses that don't fit right?"

"Sounds like the start of a Hugh Grant movie."

"I don't like him anymore. I can't watch him since the thing with that hooker."

"Why would a man like him—"

"They say it's because men—"

"Some men are just naturally—"

"In the right situation a man will—"

"Hmm. I must have 'Wrong Situation' tattooed on my ass, then," spat Pammy.

"I think that's a good idea," announced Sarah, provoking skewed looks. "Do you need adult volunteers?" She would fend off discussions of men for as long as she could.

"Oh," replied Dora. "Well, I'm sure we will. You know I'm beginning to think we can really make something of this."

"What sort of community service are we talking about?"

"Well, I was thinking...there's a proposal before the township finance committee about the funding of a recreation center—"

"Oh hell yes!" cried Pammy. "I am so tired of spending the weekends driving the little mooch monkeys around to nine different places. Forget what I said. I'm in."

"Here's to community service."

Glasses clinked. "Where better to plan the future of the world than Naked Tuesday?"

They all eased back a little further and quietly looked at the sky. Pammy broke the silence. "I have two birthdays coming up."

"Which two?"

"The two oldest. They're 362 days apart; we always celebrate together—at least until they realize they could have their own party."

"At least your boys won't have you doing hourly Google searches for Tori Tornado."

"Actually, they will."

"Maybe boys are learning not to follow gender stereotypes, finally," suggested Sarah.

"Or maybe not. Tori Tornado is something much more than a doll. I asked them why they want a girl's doll. They looked at me like I was a circus freak and said 'Link up. And swarm.' What the hell does that mean?"

····

"That one has the biggest boobs," observed Missy.

All the men looked over to verify, then nodded in agreement.

"That kid is my hero," Flip observed. "You rock," he told Missy, then slapped one of his own kids on the back of the head just for emphasis, causing the kid to blow apple juice out of his nose, in turn causing the other children to break into fits of laughter and cries of "Eeew!"

"So are we gonna do it or are we just gonna talk

about it?" Dick snapped with affected impatience.

"Oh, we're gonna do it," Flip replied.

"No, you're not. Don't be stupid. You're not going to break into someone's house," Billy corrected.

"Billy, can I get a Hooter's shirt?"

"No Missy, sorry."

"Why not?"

"'Cause your Mom would ground me and not let me watch TV for the rest of my life."

"We need to do it right, though," Flip proceeded. "And we're not breaking in like a pack of two-bit hoods. We're going to do minimal damage, and we're only going to take Tori Tornado." That last phrase was directed at Dick who wanted to leave some sort of protest message, which he claimed would be a blow for social justice. In fact, he was of the mind that someone should call the papers, believing that the average citizen would be inspired to similar heroics.

"Billy do they have Tori Tornado dolls in this mall?" asked Missy wide-eyed in hope.

"I don't think so honey, but we can check." Billy

glared at Flip who mouthed 'Sorry'.

"We need lookouts, stationed at the subdivision entrances, with walkie-talkies," Dick surmised.

"Well, Dick, there's three of us. And there are three entrances to the subdivision. Do the math."

Dick conceded after some thought. "I see. We might have to hire lackeys."

"Lackeys? You mean like guys in striped shirts and ski caps who chew on matches? What's the number to central casting?" Billy snickered.

"We're not going to hire lackeys. You make stuff too complicated and everything gets fu...fouled up. We just need to be certain he's out of the house. If we use that basement window, even if he comes back, we'll be able to escape before he catches us."

"Uh, I'm not sure how well I can fit through that window."

"Then you better lay off the hot wings," Flip retorted and moved the dish away from Dick to within reach of his kids, one of whom took the opportunity to whip an especially drippy wing into the face of his brother. With lighting reflexes the brother retaliated with a barrage of ketchup-coated French fries. The third proceeded to hose the other with a stream of lemonade emitted from his straw. Flip sprang to his feet and swiped haphazardly at the boys who easily dodged the blows by muscle memory alone.

Missy broke into an uncontrolled fit of raucous laughter.

"I have had it with you goddam animals. You pull any more of that crap and I'm gonna slap you little brats into next week! Let's go." Flip called for the check and watched closely as the waitress quickly bounced over and leaned down to place it on the table.

"I'll get it," offered Billy proffering his credit card.

"So there are three of us, right Billy?" Flip asked directly.

Billy figured that a) this would never come to fruition, and b) even if it did, they wouldn't get caught, therefore c) the whole thing would turn into an extended episode of low comedy, which would be worth it for entertainment value alone. He nodded.

"Great. Let's get the kids into the playground before

they get us banned from Hooter's for life. I've got some festivities planned."

The boys barreled into the mall playground, employing a shock-and-awe strategy toward the other children. Parental eyes widened and hands settled firmly on hips. Missy briefly attempted to keep up but eventually settled for sitting on top of a friendly plastic tortoise and watching the proceedings in amusement.

"Missy, I'm going to walk over to the Sony store, but I'll have my eye on you the whole time," said Billy.

Missy smiled, not caring as long she got to keep watching the playground morph into *Lord of the Flies*.

Once inside the Sony store, the men found themselves transfixed by 96" LCD TV on which a Pixar movie was playing. Billy reached twelve before he stopped counting speakers.

Flip picked up the remote and eyed it quizzically causing an overly earnest saleskid to approach them. "Distract him," Flip whispered. Billy and Dick positioned themselves directly in the view of the saleskid as he went into his rehearsed spiel.

They peppered the kid with softball questions about resolution and warranty and financing. In a couple of minutes Flip insinuated himself into the group and replaced the remote saying, "Guys, we gotta get back to the kids. Thanks for the info," and lead them outside taking up a position just outside the showroom window.

"What was that all about?" Dick asked.

"I think I know," replied Billy.

Missy appeared at Billy's knee shouting "Uppy!" to which Billy instantly complied. She had apparently tired of watching Flip's boys systematically reduce the other children to tears.

With a flourish, Flip displayed a contraption that could have come from a sci-fi movie prop department, but which Billy readily recognized as a universal remote.

In the store the saleskid had gone into his spiel with a new customer, a balding man in polyester slacks with a bored wife carrying three shopping bags. Flip changed the channel to some gossip show, which at the moment appeared to be running a retrospective compilation of clips of Hollywood starlet cleavage.

Every time the saleskid tried to change to the Pixar movie, Flip switched it back. In desperation he tried to turn the TV off; Flip just powered it up again.

A small pack of college-aged boys with reversed baseball caps and the sharp eyes for mischief that come with youth noticed what Flip was up to and came over to watch. One suggested he turn it to MTV where, on some juvenile Florida beach, a parade of women were presenting their very pronounced, thong-clad posteriors like troop of randy, red-assed baboons.

At each turn the saleskid's increasingly distressed attempts to abort the nightmare were countered by Flip. With the mechanical confidence of a skilled tradesman, Flip eventually placed every single TV in the shop under his nefarious control, artfully puppeteering the saleskid around the room in hopeless attempts to extinguish the soft core porn. A crowd of onlookers gathered, occasionally declaring their admiration of Flip.

And thus—with the playground in ruins, parents gathering their wailing children in their arms and heading for the exits, a hard working young fellow being tortured in confused desperation, and the masses shouting of his glory—did Flip effectively turn the JC Penney quadrant of the mall into a modern interpretation of Bosch's Bacchanalia.

••••

Three hundred yards to the west, near the Nordstrom anchor, three pretty, adolescent girls were promenading in their uniforms: scandalously low-waisted jeans beneath wispy tops that bottomed out ever so slightly above their navels. Bared abdomens were of special importance to the one of the trio who was sporting a navel ring as it marked her as more mature and sexually confident. The best the others could do were some number of toe rings which, since they were as likely to be worn by little children as they were by promiscuous harlots, were lame in comparison.

One of the two with unadorned navels was so thin that were she not as Caucasian as imaginable she could have easily passed for a famine victim. This simultaneously marked her as an object of pity, since all of her peers suspected bulimia, and envy, since they also wished they could wear size zero.

Presently, Navel-ring-girl and Famine-girl located places to sit on the edge of decorative fountain. The third girl, the most voluptuous of the three, remained standing. This was Jenna and she avoided sitting in public for she lived in mortal terror of looking fat. Instead, she periodically shifted her center of gravity, swinging her hips sensually from one side to the other when the pain in her weight-bearing heel grew intolerable.

The topic of conversation was navel rings; initiated, encouraged, and maintained by Navel-ring-girl for obvious reasons. "I know where you can get it done. I'll take you where they did mine. They won't hassle you about permission."

"My mom would kill me. Then she'd ground me. Then she'd kill me again," replied Famine-girl.

Jenna wondered briefly whether Jim would like it if she got a navel ring. It didn't matter really; there was no way she was going to draw attention to her midriff. She said nothing, her attention recaptured by her aching feet.

Various packs of teens were roving about evaluating

each other. The girls were less interested in the boys per se as they were which groups of boys were interested in them. But even more, the girls were interested in other girls: Who was surrounded by whom? Who was conspicuously violating the existing social structure? Were there any potential clique realignments and/or couple shufflings?

This evening, everyone was grouped within the acceptable parameters. Ho hum. An uncharacteristically quiet pack of boys were heading their way, taking pains to not make eye contact. At the last second the most clownish of them angled off slightly and dashed between Jenna and the seated girls, barely brushing against Jenna then turning and saying "So sorry" in a mocking tone. The boys wandered off jostling and laughing.

"Fuck off, Dickless!" called Jenna.

"Assholes!" was Navel-ring-girl's evaluation. "Look at his pants hanging halfway down his ass. What a dork. I can't believe you used to like him."

"That was like a year ago," replied an indignant Famine-girl. "He was different before he started hanging out with those youtube idiots."

"Those videos are so pathetic. I can't believe they think they're funny."

"They'll probably post one like, 'How to cop a feel from bitches at the mall'."

"Did you do it with him?" Navel-ring-girl cut to the chase.

"No! Gawd, eew! I'm sure!" cried Famine-girl, crossing her arms in front of her body in revulsion.

Jenna, with her newfound vast understanding of sex, decided that Famine-girl was a virgin, not the least reason being that if she was so totally clinically depressed that she had gone bulimic (or anorexic, or whatever) she would never have the confidence to let a boy touch her.

Now she had to sit down. She felt like the heels of her shoes had been driven through the soles of her feet and deep into her ankles. She took a seat next to Navel-ring-girl, casually placed her arms in her lap for cover, and fantasized about whipping off her shoes and soaking her feet in the central fountain. Navel-ring-girl leapt at the opportunity to poke her finger into Jenna's side and tease, "Don't try to hide it!"

"Dammit! Bitch!" snapped Jenna and she shot to her feet again.

"Oh relax," said Navel-ring-girl. "I can only do that because it's all in your head."

Jenna pursed her lips and fumed, knowing she wouldn't last much longer on her feet.

"I bet Jimbo likes it."

"Would you not call him that? I hate it when people call him Jimbo. It's vulgar."

"Oooh. Maybe we should call him James. Oh James! Kiss me James!" Navel-ring-girl was on a roll. "Did you do it with him?"

Jenna tried to sneer at her.

"Oh my god, you did! I can't believe it! Now you're a slut, you know."

"Shut up," Jenna said, with a little too much disgust.

"Jenna and Jimbo sitting in a tree..."

"Shut up!"

"Let's go into Nordstroms," suggested Famine-girl. "Will they have those blue flowered sandals I want?"

"No, those are only at Saks."

"Then let's go to Saks."

The girls resumed their promenade, Jenna's ankles going thankfully numb in self-defense.

••••

"Did you taste 'em?"

"Did you suck on 'em?"

"Fuck off," Jimbo suggested.

"Oh, there will be no off-fucking on this topic," explained the one with the premature goatee. "You cannot bang Jenna and keep it to yourself. It's your duty, man."

"I never said I banged her."

"Oh please," declared the one they called Chuckles.

"You banged Jenna. So? I thought you'd been doing that all along. What took you so long, girlie-man?" asked the one with the ferret-face.

"Let's get some pizza," suggested Chuckles.

"We just had burgers, fat ass," spat Ferret-face.

"Then let's get ice cream."

"Fuck that. I want a detailed description of Jenna's tits," demanded Premature-goatee.

"Yeah, or pictures. Oh man, did you get pics?" Ferret-face's eyes gleamed.

"No. I guess I never thought to stop and get my Nikon," Jimbo snarked.

"Four words: Cameraphone, dumbfuck."

"Let me make sure I understand. You're telling me I should have stopped in middle of everything, whipped out my phone, and had her pose for a few low-res jpegs for me to keep on my phone that I promise I won't show to anyone ever, never mind post on the Web."

"Yes, pindick. You tell her it's foreplay. Then you narrate: 'Jenna, let me see those succulent mounds of womanly delight, baby.'"

"At least tell us what they look like," pleaded Premature-goatee.

Jimbo got serious, darted his eyes about furtively, signaled for them to listen closely, and gave them a conspiratorial whisper, "They look exactly like women's breasts. I kid you not."

"Now I'm hungry again," whined Chuckles.

Unbeknownst to them, each of the boys was carrying a gene that triggered a primordial avian flocking instinct; an evolutionary remnant from epochs past. So when Jimbo rose from his seat in the Saks quadrant and entered the flow of mall traffic, the others involuntarily followed.

As they passed a series of cars on display from a local dealership (doors all locked), Chuckles looked in the window of Ford Mustang and said, "I need a job. Jimbo, can you get me a job where you work?"

"I can see if they're hiring."

"You should get a job at Fatburger for the free grease," offered Ferret-face.

"Shut up, asshole."

"Hmm. A Lincoln Navigator," observed Premature-goatee. "Jimbo, you should invest in one of these. There's enough room for you, and Jenna, and Jenna's tits."

Laughs ensued. Jimbo stopped and tried to look angry. He would have settled for indignant. The others didn't even notice, either because Jimbo was just too even-tempered to carry it off or because a random pack of comely females happened to be crossing their path, darting coy glances in their direction. The boys just outright gawked back at them.

"Follow 'em," urged Premature-goatee.

"Why?" asked Jimbo. "Are you gonna stalk them until they turn around and notice you, then hide and giggle about it?"

"No, douche-nozzle," replied Ferret-face. "We wait for the right moment and then hook up with them."

Jimbo snorted.

"Fuck you, pussywhip."

At precisely that moment, without anyone else noticing, Jimbo made perfectly serendipitous eye contact with Jenna across the mall. He made a tiny motion with his head toward the Neiman Marcus quadrant and she made an equally tiny nod of her head.

"All right," announced Jimbo in summation. "Screw you guys, I'm going home."

••••

Billy froze. Missy had run into the house ahead of him and from the foyer he heard her cry, "Hi Sarah!"

Billy fretted: Now what? Billy responded: Now nothing. It was highly unlikely they were exchanging detailed opinions of his character or scruples and plotting how to make his life a hell for not being forthright about he and Sarah's prior involvement. He put on his game face and stepped into the kitchen.

"Missy, why don't you—Oh. Hello, Sarah."

Missy was sitting in Sarah's lap and grinning playfully. Sarah smiled inscrutably at Billy.

"Guess where we went," queried Missy, bouncing in excitement.

"You didn't—" said Marlene.

"Hooters!" announced Missy.

Billy got double-barreled baleful stares from the adult women.

"It was her suggestion," Billy offered; secretly glad to have this be the scandal of the evening.

"Really? And I suppose then you had ice cream for dinner at her suggestion?"

"Nope. We had wings and beer!" interjected Missy.

Deeper stares ensued.

"She didn't have beer."

"Yes I did."

"No you didn't, Missy."

"I did when you weren't looking. I drank your glass and the waitress filled it up when you weren't looking."

"She didn't have beer," he said to Marlene.

"Then I guess the evening was a success," came the arid reply.

"I think I'm going to get going," said Sarah, gently kissing Missy and setting her down. "So maybe I'll see you on Wednesday night?"

"Unless something comes up. Sarah has convinced me to come to her yoga class."

Billy instantly remembered Midge, and that he had not yet called her. He instinctively reached for his cell phone. Catching himself mid-flip, he just regarded it thoughtfully as if he were checking for messages. "That sounds great."

••••

The little blond boys stampeded for the remote control.

Flip shouted, "No TV!" and was summarily ignored as the battle for the remote began. One boy managed to get control, another frustrated his ambitions by repeatedly positioning himself to block the signals, the third, and most historically knowledgeable, broke off to use the controls on the TV set itself.

Flip walked into the kitchen where Pammy, clad in her frumpy bathrobe and yellow terrycloth slippers, was casually awaiting the point where she would chase the kids off into the basement to fight over the Playstation while she watched what she wanted.

"Fun dinner?"

"Yeah it was fine, nothing special. Did you have fun with the girls?"

"We all got naked in the hot tub and talked about how horny we are." She smiled suggestively at Flip. He smiled back.

"So where'd you eat?" Pammy asked.

Flip's smile evaporated. "Goddammit!" he shouted at the kids and dashed into the living room to chase them away from the TV.

Pammy's face hardened. "Now Flip, Dora is making arrangements for a community project. She is going to try to get a recreation center funded and she needs petition signatures."

"Oh Jesus Christ why? Why?" Flip wailed from the next room.

"Stop that. Dora is our friend and she is having a hard time, so we're going to help her."

"Of course, by 'we' you mean me."

"No, I mean both of us. I'm going to help her see to the permit details. You are going to help with the Youth Advocate Program."

"Please...I'm begging you..."

"Stop it. Look, we're going to have the kids go around and collect signatures as a way for them to learn about community service. All you have to do is go along with them—"

"For the love of God, no."

"—and supervise."

"Let's see. The best possible outcome is that I have to stand around with my thumb up my ass as the kids learn valuable skills for their future careers as door-to-door salesmen. More likely I'll spend the whole day chasing them down while they run in three different directions at once, destroy everything in sight, and annoy the piss out of the entire neighborhood who, by the way, we are trying to get to sign a petition for the good of the children."

He turned and Pammy was standing facing him, steely eyed and with her robe open unnaturally wide at the top. Flip looked her in the chest. Pammy noticed. Flip turned away quickly.

Pammy seethed. "How about you be useful for something, at least? Look, you just walk around, engage the neighbors in a little small talk, get them to sign the petition—they will, they have no reason not to—and move on. Even if the kids are complete savages, they're still children—you won't be refused. I'll arrange for Billy to go with you to help keep the kids on a leash. Stop with the wincing. It's not like you're asking for money, like with the fountain."

Slowly Flip's grimace disappeared and a certain gleam appeared in his eye. "Fine," he said. "I'll talk to Billy and we'll arrange a day."

"You'll arrange a week from today. Never mind, I'll do it.   Everyone is getting mobilized for next Saturday. We're going to canvas the entire neighborhood on that day."

"Sure, Hon," Flip said genially. "A week from today. No problem."

Under Pammy's wary gaze Flip slouched away and into the recliner, lost in thought as the battle for the remote raged around him.

••••

It was likely the first time in months that Dick and Dora were alone together. Dora's response to this was to speak more formally than usual and carefully guard against any friendly familiarities that might seep into the conversation. Dick acknowledged this by doing what he always did: validate her emotions and honor her wishes.

"We are aiming for a week from Saturday to gather signatures," announced Dora.

"Well, sure."

"Most people are pairing up—an adult or two and some children. Jenna can go with her little friend Jim and take little Missy along. So you need to find someone to team up with."

"Well, once you get the signatures we have to go before the community outreach committee at the school board and expand our reach, don't we?"

"Yes."

"Well, I am an educator. Well, all I'm suggesting is that my assignment be on that end of things."

"You're saying you don't want to go out a week from Saturday."

"Well, no. But I just thought it would be better off if I handled something more administrative."

"If that's how you feel, all right. Everyone else is doing it though."

"Are you?"

"No!" Dora snapped defensively. "I am going to coordinate from a central location. I'd like to use our...the basement." She paused to shake off the miscue, then added, "If that's OK."

"Well, of course...but, you see...I was really wondering if I could pair up with you. Or maybe both of us could go with Jenna and Missy. I'm sure Jimbo has other things to do. Like work, I mean."

Dora regarded Dick with a combination of compassion and suspicion.

Dick continued. "Well, what I mean is...you see...I know you have some anger towards me...so I understand...but I think it would be helpful if we—

the three of us—spent a little time together now and then. That is, I think it would be good for Jenna."

"I'm not ang...I don't think Jenna would like that. She and I don't really communicate very well anymore." Tears began to well in Dora's eyes.

Dick spoke quietly. "I don't think she's said more than five words at a time to me since you left. Maybe if we spent some time together—I mean, now and then—we could reconnect."

"She's got a whole life," cried Dora. "She got a whole life going on and I don't know a thing about it. She must think I am a terrible person. Terrible for leaving."

"She doesn't think that."

"Yes she does! I know she does! Oh, how did I lose my little girl?"

The faucet opened full blast. Dick tentatively grasped her hand. "No, she doesn't think that. She's just a teenager and that's what teenagers do. They separate from their parents. They work their way out of the nest. We just need to find a way to be a part of it."

"Oh, Dick, I miss...her so much."

"Shhh. It's OK hon."

But as Dick moved closer Dora's defenses kicked in and she pulled away and began to wipe her eyes. "Just quit it, alright? Listen, if you don't want to go a week from Saturday—"

"No, no—I'll go. Maybe with Flip or Billy."

Dora moved to leave. At the door she turned back and said, "Maybe once this is over we can see about getting together with Jenna."

....

The key portions of Jenna's and Jimbo's anatomy remained uncovered as they lay side by side behind the equipment shed in back of the school. Jenna was completely indifferent to the vaguely itchy sensation of the grass on her bare behind. Jimbo's right calf had gone into spasm almost instantly after he climaxed and he was absentmindedly massaging it back to normal. Their long, deep, quiet breaths moved in and out of synchronization, each one highlighting the awareness of muscles fatigued from exertion. It was a sensation of serenity and fulfillment that neither had known before, yet each would endlessly pursue throughout the remainder of their lives.

The mosquitoes, unimpressed with the post-coital aura and immodest about the exposed portions of their bodies, feasted heartily. Jimbo sat up first. He removed the condom and tossed it aside. Jenna sat up next after finding her panties and slipping them on while still reclined. As Jimbo re-belted his pants Jenna whispered sternly, "You can't just throw that there."

"What? What do you want me to do?"

"I don't know, but I'm sure latex isn't biodegradable." She pulled her shirt down over her breasts.

"You want me to take it to the recycling center?"

Jenna's phone rang. The ringtone was the beginning of the Patsy Cline song "Walking After Midnight," which she knew as a TV commercial jingle from when she was about ten years old. "Hello...yes...I'm at the mall...what...what are you...when...no...yes... no...I'll see...Mom, I'll see...OK...OK...bye...OK...bye...OK what?" With an epic eye-roll, Jenna set the phone down on the grass still open. It emitted a steady stream of shrill and strident clamor as Jenna stood up and shimmied into her jeans. She noticed Jimbo's bemusement at the scene and favored him with a sloppy kiss. Only then did she reach down and pick up the still squawking phone. "OK...yeah...no...Mom, I have to go...nowhere..."

Jimbo slipped his arms around her from behind.

"OK bye...BYE!" Jenna snapped the phone shut.

"Was that just the usual?"

"No, she wants us to go door-to-door with Missy a week from Saturday."

"Door-to-door what?"

"Collecting signatures for some stupid thing. Apparently children are unrefusable salesmen."

"What?"

"Walking After Midnight" chimed again. Jenna's scowled at the neon blue caller ID.

She slipped the phone unanswered into her purse. "Now my dad. I don't know what it is. Just, whatever. Do you have another condom?"

Jimbo sighed, "No." He let his arms fall from around Jenna.

••••

"Pammy," Marlene told Billy, looking at her called ID.

Billy flipped open his ringing cell. "Flip," he said with a snort.

They exchanged bemused smiles and Billy walked out on to the porch. Marlene slipped the phone from its cradle.

"Hello."

"I told Flip he could take Billy with him a week from Saturday. Do you think that will be OK?"

"Sure. I think Billy is finding that out now."

"They went to Hooters didn't they?"

"Of course."

"I wouldn't mind if I thought it would get me some tonight."

Marlene withheld both sympathetic and empathetic comments. She looked over at Missy who was finally running out of steam for the evening. The thought of getting her in her bedclothes, the inevitable minor resistance to brushing her teeth, and the associated negotiation to read to her if she did, wearied Marlene as much as the actions themselves would. She just couldn't summon the energy to engage Pammy in a bitch session. "I suppose. Although uninterrupted sleep has a lot of appeal," she replied, accepting that it would cement Pammy's view of her as selfish and unsisterly.

"Hmm. Well, you get your rest. Bye, Mar," replied Pammy, taking the hint as politely as possible. "Some people just have to be superior, don't they?" she told the open refrigerator.

••••

"Hey, Flip."

"A week from Saturday."

"What?"

"Recon."

"What?"

"I'll fill you in later, just be prepared for a week from Saturday. Don't make any plans."

"What?"

"Just don't tell anybody."

"What?"

"As far as anyone knows, we're being good citizens for Dora's dumb-ass jack-off project."

"What?"

"Later." Click.

Billy regarded the phone. He had no doubt that wanton stupidity of the highest order was in his future. He suddenly began scrolling through his call log for Midge's number. Finding it he clicked dial and instantly regretted it. Stuck now, unable to disconnect without his name appearing in her call log, he waited, praying she would not answer. Blessedly, her voice mail took the call. "Hi Midge, it's Billy. Sorry it's taken so long to call back. Just wanted to check in and see..." Billy struggled to stop himself from a perfectly natural "if you wanted to get together again," instead grasping for something without intent, "...what was going on with you," and grimacing at the sound of it. He then paused too long, giving the impression of discomfort, and closed with "I guess I'll talk to you later," certain, as he always was, that he sounded like an absolute doofus on voice mail.

Looking back at the lights in the house, Billy was, for the moment, content to be dissociated. He knew he had to honestly believe that he was going to have more than perfunctory sex with Marlene, lest the anxiety over his recent pathetic performances become self-fulfilling. He was not quite ready to go the Viagra route yet. Somehow that seemed like cheating. A few more such dismal attempts and Marlene would be insulted and would decide there was a "problem" and then there would be "talks." How was he supposed to perform with that possibility hanging over him? Now, maybe if he was to seduce Midge—the exotic, unfamiliar Midge...would bedding her reconfirm his virility and rejuvenate him? Oh, the danger and passionate abandon of possessing such a sweet young thing. Maybe it would work, if he was careful enough not to make any references to '80s sitcoms.

At the end of the street he saw a bright light streaming from Otto's basement window. What a fantastic and bizarre world was this place called the suburbs. Shaking his head lightly, he started sharply as he turned to see Dick standing immediately behind him.

"Christ, Dick, what are you, a ninja?"

Dick didn't respond, other than by extending an index finger in the air as a universal symbol of pause. He was listening intently to his phone with furrowed brow. "Jenna. No answer," he intoned.

Billy looked at his watch; barely 11PM. Not really surprising that she was not home yet. "Does she have a curfew?"

"No, no. We, well...we don't believe in teaching children to submit to arbitrary rules."

"She's probably hanging out with Jimbo."

Dick looked at Billy, momentarily thinking that may have been a ribald comment. Billy looked as innocent as he was. "So she can't answer her phone?"

"That's how teenagers are, I guess. They believe parents are only a marginal reality. Weren't you like that as a teenager?" he asked in response to Dick's quizzical look.

"Oh, well. I was...well...no I was...well, I never spent all that much time out. My friends usually just went to each other's house to watch TV—*The A-Team, Magnum P.I.*; you know, action shows."

"Oh." Billy nodded, careful to betray no hint of pity. He turned back to look at Otto's house again. The basement light was still cleaving the night like a spotlight. "Do you know anything about recon?"

"Recon what?"

"That's what I said."

Dick's phone rang. "Jenna? Oh, Flip. What? Saturday? Recon what?"

PART 3

Hijinks Ensue

September 22

At 3:59AM Sarah awoke and sat up gracefully. Without a glance, she reached back and shut off the alarm microseconds after the clock began to flash 4AM. She sat crossed-legged in the dark silence gathering her thoughts, which did not include going back to sleep even for just five more minutes. She moved through her morning grooming and green tea ritual without affectation or expression and, as usual, discovered she had nearly twenty minutes before she had to leave. She left anyway and used the time to stop at Krispy Kreme for a cruller.

The donut was one of two things that kept her

interest while she led her sunrise Yoga class through a series of standard postures. It was not nauseating, but she was aware of its disharmonious presence in her stomach. At times it drove her to leave a pose and weave among her students, offering a kindly "Remember to find your comfort zone and relax into it; no two people look the same in any pose," and gently correcting the positions of the most awkward.

She was paying special attention to the second thing that occupied her mind: a new student; a lovely, youthful Asian girl. After the final "Namaste," Sarah gave Dora a don't-go-anywhere hand signal and moved deftly between the three lingering men that were waiting for an opening to chat her up.

"Hi. I don't think I've seen you here before, have I?"

"No, it's my first time."

"Well, welcome. I'm Sarah."

"Midge."

"Is this your first yoga class?"

"Yeah, well, no. I mean, I've done a couple of tapes —"

"You did very well. You must have a dance background or gymnastics—"

"Yeah, I was on the dance squad in high school when I was young."

"Have you been a member here long?"

"Almost a year, I guess."

"Well it was good to have you in class. I hope you come back, I think you have a real talent for it."

"Thanks, I probably will."

Sarah moved back to Dora. By this time there was only one man left, self-consciously doing some supplemental stretching.

"So did you enjoy yourself?"

"Oh, yes," replied Dora, who was thoroughly sweat-stained. "There were some things I just couldn't seem to do, though."

"That's not important, as long as you feel better. Everything comes in time."

"I should do this more. I should do it twice a week; it might help with my weight. Does it burn a lot of calories?"

"It can, but the more important thing is the body awareness you get. The more familiar you get with what your body is telling you, the better your overall health."

"Do you wanna go get a Starbucks?"

"I don't think I can right now, I have another class to teach at nine, and I'll end up having to pee half way through."

"Oh, well."

Sarah didn't want to do it. She knew she would regret it. But the pause left no option. "Is there something bothering you?"

"Do you think I should go back to Dick?"

"Did he ask you?"

"No."

"Does he want to?"

"I don't know. He never wanted to divorce in the first place."

"Do you want to?"

"I don't know."

"Maybe we should get together sometime and talk," Sarah suggested gently fanning herself with her loose fitting t-shirt indicating she was too sweaty to keep talking. "Better yet, when we see Marlene and Pammy this afternoon, maybe we could make time for a group confab over it. I mean, once the signatures are all gathered."

"That'd be nice."

"OK, I'll see you later at Dick's; don't let anything get you down, these things have a way of sorting themselves out," Sarah offered a reassuring smile and a friendly grasp of Dora's arm then headed off to the locker room before the last man in the room could approach her. Glancing back, she saw the last man had struck up a conversation with Dora instead.

••••

Many months later, a man was searching Google for the address of a Chinese restaurant that happened to be a about a mile down the main thoroughfare from a normal-looking neighborhood with a little cul-de-sac that desperately needed a fountain. Rather than just retrieve the address, Google provided him with a full satellite image of the surrounding area and alternative dining options within a radius of ten miles including customer reviews and, in a couple of cases, news articles about health violations. If the man had looked closely enough at the image, he would have made out little clutches of ant-like dots congregated at various positions across the neighborhood. Some were positioned in front of houses. Some were elongated, indicating motion in concert.

Missy, perhaps unsurprisingly, knew what a satellite was and even had a solid enough understanding of Google that had she known one was overhead she would have been shouting and waving her arms gleefully to the skies. Instead, she was banking minutes on the swings. To avoid any sort of drama, Jenna had struck a deal early on which provided Missy with two minutes of time on the swings for each signature they got.

"How many now?"

"Six minutes," Jenna replied.

"Is that almost an hour?"

"Not yet."

"How many minutes is almost an hour?"

"Twenty." Jenna looked at Jimbo, who shrugged.

"I want to play on the swings for almost an hour."

"OK, Sweetie, then let's keep going."

"How many more until we have almost an hour?"

"Seven."

"Oh! Why can't we go to the swings now?"

"Not yet, we need more signatures."

"But why can't we go now?"

"Are you ready? Here." Jenna handed the clipboard to Missy and rang the doorbell. They were an effective team. Between Missy's pleading little voice and Jenna's halter top they made short work of everyone except the most bitter of old women, and those eventually succumbed to Jimbo's polite respectfulness and willingness to make agreeable statements about how disrespectful most young people are these days.

The instant the team had achieved "almost an

hour" of swing time, Missy made a beeline for the playground. Jenna and Jimbo quickened their pace to keep up. Upon sighting the little neighborhood park across the street, Missy darted away at full speed. Jimbo lunged forward and caught her before she blindly ran out in front of a passing car, admonishing patiently, "Missy, always look both ways, OK?" As soon as the car passed Missy pulled out of his grip and made for the swings.

Jenna took Jimbo's hand and held it until he was required to push Missy "Really, really, really high!" When Missy had moved on to the monkey bars, Jimbo took a seat next to Jenna on a park bench and Jenna took his hand again. And when Missy periodically cried, "Watch me! Watch me!" they replied with warm encouragement and smiled at her in peaceful satisfaction.

Strange emotions washed over Jenna. She forgot about her aversion to sitting and even allowed her shoulders to slump ever so slightly, thoughtlessly confident in her emotional partnership with Jim and her matronly connection with Missy. Was it a form of pride she was taking in Missy? Was it her ease and contentment with Jim? Reverie, she might call it. She became aware of the air filling her lungs with each breath. Her attention had moved outside herself. She conceptualized the scene from afar. She sensed she was very close to experiencing a feeling she had not known since the onset of puberty: Gratitude. She did not want it to end, whatever it was.

"Walking After Midnight" broke the spell.

"Hello...Oh Mom...I don't know, about ten...Yes, that's all...No...No...No." Jenna snapped the phone shut and grimaced.

"No. No. No. No. No," mocked Missy, giggling.

••••

"Put Jenna down for ten, I guess."

Dora was belligerently swaggering about, absent-mindedly wielding a plastic toy light saber like a martinet with a riding crop. Her shoulders were back, her carriage was confident, her gaze steely and unflinching, her inflection did not allow for dissent. The troops were in action and she was monitoring progress closely from the basement of

Dick's house. Marlene was fielding phone calls from the individual team leaders and recording the number of signatures on gridded paper, amusedly accommodating the newly possessed Dora by vocally updating a running total with each new report. Sarah was in charge of the map. In theory, she would track the progress of the various teams across the neighborhood, using pushpins of specific colors, and identify any side streets or cul-de-sacs that were neglected. Pammy would then redeploy the patrols accordingly.

But Sarah was more concerned with the Last Man. For some reason, that yoga straggler that Dora had been talking with after class was now here at headquarters. Why did Dora invite him? Was he working to get Dora to put in a good word for him? His name was Ted, which sat poorly with Sarah for some reason. Ted: a deceptive name if there ever was one. She suspected he was a Republican, or possibly a Mormon—or both. He had a round, blatantly Anglo-Saxon face and a ten dollar haircut under which he showed early signs of balding. Khakis and penny loafers. For some reason he was the only one to whom Dora had not assigned a task, so he was just a hovering presence, making the smallest possible talk with everyone.

"You know I never get a chance to tell you how much I enjoy your class."

"Oh, well, thank you. That's nice of you to say."

"Have you been teaching long?"

"A few years now."

He spoke very blandly to her, as if he was trying to emphasize how incidental the conversation was. There was a bit of an extended pause as he waited to see if she would extend the conversation with a reciprocal question. She didn't and he went over to talk to Pammy.

"Where in God's name is Dick?" snapped Dora.

On cue, Flip, Billy and Dick strode in, Flip's kids in tow.

"What have you been doing?" cried Dora, rhetorically. "Do you know we have been working at this all afternoon and you have done nothing?"

"Well, we are going to do something now, don't you worry," responded Dick transparently.

"This is Ted," Pammy said. Ted was getting savagely

pummeled by the trio of blonde boys, but he managed to get to his feet to shake hands.

"Good to meet you. Do you live around here?" asked Billy ingratiatingly.

"Nearby, I just—"

"Why are you here? Are you a cop? A Fed?" Flip quizzed suspiciously.

"Um, no, I'm in cement."

Cement, that must be exciting, thought Sarah.

"Cement. That's heavy, man," Flip replied, deeming him a non-entity.

"Forgive him," Pammy interjected. "He's afflicted with terminal dumbass."

"I asked Ted to help out. I met him in Sarah's yoga class," Dora announced.

Dick eyed him up and down.

"Exactly when were you all planning on making a contribution? Or are you just going to waste the day like always?" Dora asked, nearly achieving sarcasm.

"We're going right now," replied Flip. He indicated the area on the map to Sarah then gathered up his boys by the hair.

As they exited, Billy gave Marlene a smile and a shrug.

....

"A coke drinking contest. That's how I know."

"What?"

"About twenty minutes ago we had a coke drinking contest." Flip beamed as his boys tussled violently in disagreement over who won.

"Jesus, Flip! You caffeinated them? Are you crazy?" cried Billy.

"Just as crazy as I need to be."

The whole group was walking directly down the middle of the street, passing assigned houses with every few steps, zeroing in on Otto's house.

"Who was that guy Dora invited?" asked Dick.

"Ted," answered Billy.

"What kind of a name is that?" asked Dick.

"First, I think," answered Billy.

"It's my house; she should have asked before inviting a stranger, shouldn't she?" asked Dick.

"Bad manners," answered Billy.

"Have you ever taken Yoga?" asked Dick.

"Only to meet girls," answered Billy, instantly regretting it.

"Why the hell would Dora want to take up yoga?" asked Dick.

"Maybe she's trying to get her legs behind her head so Ted can bang her silly," answered Flip.

"Flip!" cried Billy.

Dick stared in shock.

"Kidding. I'm kidding. What are you so upset about? Just kidding. Look, Dick, don't worry, the guy's clearly a zero. He's in cement, what the fuck is that? He's like a hamburger and you're like...a chuck roast, or something—I don't know. I was kidding. C'mon, you guys, the time bomb is about to go off."

Billy spoke to Dick aside, "Look, don't listen to that. You're jumping to conclusions."

"What, I'm not...I don't care. It's none of my business. We don't have any claims on each other."

They covered more ground, shepherding the kids along as best they could. Dick eventually broke the silence. "Look at this bastard," he offered as they passed the trash cans that had been so ill-treated. "Plastic, aluminum—in the trash. Who doesn't recycle anymore? Answer me that."

All three of Flip's children were holding their crotches and grimacing. Flip smiled at his handiwork. "You guys need to pee?"

"Yes!" they all screamed.

"OK, we'll ask the man in this house if you can use his bathroom."

They trudged up to Otto's front door, senses ablaze with the anticipation of the caper. Flip rang the doorbell while his children were running in circles and moaning. In time, Otto opened the door.

"Hi, Otto, do you m—"

Flip did not get a chance to finish. The boys dashed through the open door in a panic of biological necessity. Otto barely got out a "Hey" in protest before the boys were ping-ponging all about his house in search of a bathroom.

Flip said, "Sorry about that. I hope you don't mind if they use your bathroom. Kids and their little bladders, eh?"

"Well, I guess so," answered Otto.

"Very magnanimous," intoned Dick behind a baleful stare as they all stepped inside.

"So Otto, we're collecting signatures, would you mind?" said Flip pushing a clipboard in front of him.

"Signatures for what?"

"For what? Oh, for a fountain in the cul-de-sac..."

Otto's brow furrowed. He grinned nervously.

"...just kidding! It's for a recreation center, you know, for the children."

"Why wo—" Otto was interrupted by series of ascending screeches from the children who had managed to find their way upstairs and were almost certainly doing something unspeakable.

"I better go get them," said Flip, handing the clipboard to Billy and pushing past Otto.

"Um, so Otto, are you interested in signing?" Billy asked.

"I'd rather not."

"Uh huh," intoned Dick, his jowls seeming growing more prominent by the minute.

"Are you sure? It's just to get this before the council. There's no obligation to do anything, really," continued Billy.

One child—now liberated by an empty bladder —darted downstairs and slid between the men, sprinting for Otto's kitchen. Otto frowned even deeper and offered another mild "Hey."

"I notice you don't recycle," Dick started in. "Is there some reason for that?"

"I don't find there to be much benefit—" Otto was cutoff this time by Flip returning from upstairs carrying the remaining two children, one under each arm. Dropping them on the floor he asked, "Where's their brother?"

Billy pointed to the kitchen.

"Dammit! What are you doing in there?" Flip cried in mock anger and stomped off kitchenward while the recently dropped children scattered.

"Otto," Dick resumed. "About recycling. Just what is the issue there?"

"You see," started Otto. "I don't think the cost is worth the benefit."

"Huh? What are you talking about? There's no benefit? What kind of—"

"Hey," again Otto offered protest to the child who was violently manipulating the buttons on his DVD player.

"What's going on out there?" shouted Flip from the kitchen.

The third child instantly darted around the corner towards Otto's bedroom. Otto could only repeat, "Hey."

"Is it too much hassle for you? Is that it?" asked Dick.

"What?" replied Otto.

"Recycling. Is it the hassle or do you just not care?"

"I—"

A child emerged from bedroom carrying a Playboy magazine. He walked up to Otto and said, "Uh-oh.

You could get a boner from this you know."

Otto snatched the magazine away. "Look, you're going to have to lea—"

"Hey! Get back here!" Flip, emerging from the kitchen with another child under his arm, shouted at the boy who ran giggling back toward the bedroom.

"Wow, that's got to be from the early '70s," Billy observed about the magazine. "Are you a collector?"

"You could say that," replied Otto. "Now look you really should be—"

Flip interrupted again, "You: Get your hands off that! Don't touch that DVD again or I will kill you. Understand? And you: sit here and don't move again. If you move from that seat I will kill you." He then dashed around towards the bedroom to gather the last of his spawn.

"Don't like kids much either, do you, Otto?" Dick taking a new tack on Otto's reprehensibility.

Billy sensed it was time to close. "Sorry about all the interruption, Otto. Hey, look on the bright side. If we can get this rec center going, the kids will be that much further away from you on the weekends."

Billy gave his most ingratiating smile. Otto thought for a second, then signed the petition.

Flip reappeared and chivvied all of his children out the front door, followed by Billy who said, "Thanks, Otto" and Dick who said, "Sorry we didn't provide anything of value."

When they reached the street and Otto had triple locked the door behind them, Flip just said, "Mission accomplished."

••••

"Well, I guess congratulations are in order, Jenna," Dora deadpanned. "Your whopping ten signatures are not the lowest total after all. In fact, it's exactly ten times more than your father."

Dick offered a knowing nod and a cryptic, "Oh, we did OK."

Dora ignored him; she was in charge of everything and had no time for such trivialities. "Despite that, it looks like we have enough signatures. Thank you everybody for your help. Now Ted and I have to go and look over the potential site. I'll see you all later."

Ted leapt to his feet as soon as he realized he was supposed to follow her, offering a friendly, "Nice meeting everyone," as he left.

There was an extended pause then Dick announced "Well. I have things to do. Jenna, lock up if you leave before I come back."

There was another awkward pause.

"Alright you guys, let's get going. Get moving now." Pammy made her good-byes and Flip followed her out, herding the children ahead of him.

"Thanks, for looking after Missy, Jenna. And you too Jim," Marlene offered as she picked up Missy and headed for home with Billy.

Jenna and Jimbo looked at each other in the sudden absence of people. They managed to have sex in her bed in three different positions, including a two previously untried, before Dick returned.

September 25

Marlene rises instantly to the 5:45 alarm. No snoozing. Billy kisses her absent-mindedly and goes back to sleep.

She nearly trips over the wreckage on the floor of her daughter's room and shakes Missy awake.

"Time to get up, sweetie."

Missy snarls and turns away.

"Honey, come on."

Missy snarls and turns away.

"Get up, Missy."

Missy snarls and turns away.

"Get up now!"

Missy snarls and turns away. Marlene lifts her out of bed and drags her into the bathroom.

"No—too hot!"

Marlene adjusts the water temperature.

"No—too cold!"

Marlene adjusts the water temperature.

"No—still cold!"

Marlene adjusts the water temperature.

"No—too hot!"

Marlene pulls Missy into the shower. Missy bawls earnestly.

"Missy, you can't wear that shirt, it's dirty."

"But I want to wear it."

"You can't until I wash it."

"Can you wash it now?"

"No honey, there's not enough time."

"But why didn't you wash it before?"

"I'm sorry sweetie. Why don't you put on your blue lace shirt?"

"But I want to wear this one."

"You can't honey, it's dirty. I'll wash it tonight you can wear it tomorrow."

"But why didn't you wash it if you knew I wanted to wear it?"

"Missy I don't have time to argue. Wear the blue one."

"No. I hate that shirt."

"Missy we don't have time, put the shirt on now."

"You hate me."

Marlene sets a bowl of frosted corn flakes in front of Missy and starts answering email and drinking coffee. Missy gets up and walks to the refrigerator.

"Missy what are you doing."

"I want macaroni and cheese."

"You can't have macaroni and cheese for breakfast."

"Why?"

"Because it's not good for breakfast."

"Why?"

"Missy I don't have time make it. Just eat your cereal."

Missy accidentally knocks a couple Tupperware containers on the floor.

"Missy there is no macaroni and cheese in the fridge. It has to be made."

"Then will you make it?"

"No. There isn't any time. Eat your cereal."

Missy grabs a package of hot dog and struggles to open it.

"Give me that. Melissa!"

"I want hot dogs!"

"No! Melissa, eat your cereal!"

"I hate cereal!"

"Fine." Marlene drops the bowl cereal in the sink and puts the hot dogs back in the fridge and the spilled Tupperware containers back on the shelves with her right hand, without spilling the mug of coffee in her left.

"Missy what are you doing?"

"Playing Reader Rabbit."

"Missy I was working on that laptop! Did you... Never mind. Go put your shoes on."

Missy does not react.

"Missy! Your shoes! Now!" Marlene closes the laptop.

"No! I want Reader Rabbit!"

"Get your shoes on this instant Melissa! This instant!" Marlene is now screeching.

They exit the house and Billy staggers downstairs wondering why they have to be so noisy in the morning.

"Put your seatbelt on."

"No! You hate me!"

"Missy. I don't hate you, but we don't have time. You

have to go to school."

"I don't wanna go to school!"

"Put your seatbelt on."

"I don't wanna go to school!"

"Put your seatbelt on!"

Marlene unbuckles her seatbelt to buckle Missy's. Missy reaches to unbuckle it.

"Melissa if you unbuckle that I am going to take you out into the middle of the street and spank you in front of the whole neighborhood. Do you want that? You are being horrible. Just horrible! If this is how you behave in school no wonder you are getting in trouble. You are going to have to start behaving properly, do you understand me! I'm not going to keep putting up with this!"

Missy cries the entire way to school and slams the car door as she exits.

Marlene has her Blackberry tight to her ear. "OK, can you fill me in right now? Yes. No, I'm in traffic; there's an accident or something. I'll try, but I'm stuck dead. Can you tell me what they responded to our propo...I-94. Yes. Well, I didn't know. I must have missed the traffic announcement. Listen, I was under the impression they were going to respond...Chad...Chad...I'm glad you were prepared, but I didn't know there would be construction...Thank you Chad; I'll remember that for tomorrow. But can you tell me what the response was to our proposal. It was supposed to arrive this morning. Did anything come this morning? Are you sure? Nothing? Did you look through today's deliveries? All right I'll call over there to see...I don't know, it depends on traffic. Well, I may be a little later than nine. I know, I know —I was supposed to bring donuts this morning. I will bring them, but I may be a little late...Well, tomorrow I will know what route to take to avoid the traffic but right now I am stuck and I can't change that, do you see how that works?"

"Eight left? Four maple almond. Four of the strawberry frosted. Yeah, thanks." Marlene is back on her Blackberry. "Hello...Hi Jane, it's Marlene, how are you? Fine, I wanted to ask you...no, that's what

I was calling about. We didn't receive it, I was just checking to see if there was a problem...Oh you did? Well, that's fine, I'm sure it'll come later...No, that's OK...really, no...you don't need to check. I can—"

Marlene covers the mic. "Just mix up another dozen, I really don't care what they are."

"Jane you didn't have to check...when? Who signed for it? OK, then the miscommunication is on my end. Jane I'm so sorry to bother you, I've had a mess of a morning and I haven't even made it to the office yet. I'm sure it's there...no don't...don't resend it. I don't want you to go to any trouble OK. I'll sort it out...like I said I'm sure the problem is on my end."

"Chad...Listen I just got off the phone with...Chad, I have the donuts...No, I'm not going to make nine o'clock. There's been an accident and traffic is slow...Chad, I was just talking to Jane and she said they...Chad, I will bring the donuts, I will get there as soon as I can, now listen: I just got off the phone with Jane and they said they sent the proposal and that it arrived and you signed for it...Fed Ex, Chad, they track packages. Yesterday, Chad. Did you sign for a package yesterday?"

Marlene tries to squeeze into the left lane but no one is letting her in. She darts out in front of someone and gets the horn. The left lane stops and the right lane begins moving.

"So why did you tell me it didn't come? You have to be joking! Did you really think that when I asked if it came today I only wanted to know if it came this morning? Did you think if it came yesterday I didn't want to know about it? What the fu...I am stuck behind an accident. Chad, would you find the package and set it on the desk in my office? Do you think you can do that? Because I looked like an idiot calling about something that had arrived already. Chad, I will be there as soon as I can, will you see that the package is on my desk when I get there? Good."

Marlene hangs up. Traffic is stopped dead. She turns off the radio and turns off the ignition and rests her head on the wheel. After a moment she opens one of the boxes of donuts and eats hers. Then she eats Chad's.

At lunchtime Marlene maneuvers carefully through a parking structure at the mall, deftly dodging drivers blindly backing out and she looks for a parking spot where the neighboring SUVs have left enough room to open the door. She plans to pick up a gift certificate at Gap Kids for Pammy's boys, who have a birthday coming up, then stop at the ATM, then pick up a skirt she had left at the cleaners, then get back to work within 45 minutes all the while finding time to get a bite of food.

"Hello...Oh, hello Principal Zimmerman, is everything alright? Is Missy OK? What sort of difficulty? I'm sure she didn't mean it; I'll talk to her when...that doesn't make any sense, why would you...I understand you *can* do it, but why *would* you...what are you talking about 'charges?' Oh, for chrissakes. Listen, let me make an appointment with her teacher...You can't let her stay until the end of the day? I can't just stop everything and rush over...so make her sit in the principal's office...OK... OK...OK, I'll get there as soon as I can..."

The ATM is temporarily down for maintenance and a little handwritten sign informs her that they regret the inconvenience, but please see a teller. Inside the branch office there are thirteen people in line and one of the two tellers who were working just put the "next window please" sign up. Marlene gets back on the phone.

"Billy, it's me. I need a favor. I need you to pick up Missy from school. I'm sorry to call you at work. But I don't think I can get there and they say she needs to be taken home. Call me back right away if you can so I can tell the school that you are coming to get her. Ok, bye."

"Jenna, it's Marlene. Is there any chance you can come right over after school? I have to get Missy out early and if can leave her with you as soon as you get over, I might be able to get back to work for a couple of hours. Call me. Bye."

The line decreases by one; a new customer drops a set of two-inch thick ledgers on the counter in from of the teller and starts at the beginning. Marlene gives up and leaves.

Marlene hands her dry cleaning ticket to the clerk and checks her watch. She makes a call. "Chad, I have to go get my daughter at school. Can you reschedule this afternoon's meeting? I can probably make it back by four. I know...tell him I'm sorry but there has been trouble with my...You don't have to explain it to him, just reschedule the me...Tell him I asked you to. Why would he do that, Chad? My daughter...yes...Chad, it's fine. Just reschedule. It doesn't matter what conference room, whichever one is open...No don't tell anyone why, they don't care, they just need to know it has been rescheduled. Can't you just...Chad, just find a meeting room and send a notice, that's all! Can you do that? Thank you."

The dry-cleaning clerk returns with the skirt and, not having sufficient cash, Marlene fumbles through her purse for a credit card when her phone rings. Purse on knee, searching with right hand, her left hand wedges the Blackberry securely between her neck and tilted head.

"Billy, thank God. Can you pick up Missy at school, she has to come home." Marlene hands her Visa to the clerk. "No she's not sick she's...can you hold on a second?" Marlene completes the transaction, re-pockets her card and slings the skirt over her shoulder and exits.

"She apparently used some kind of bad language...I think it was worse than poopy-head. They say she's suspended for the time being. No, I'm dead serious.

They talk about pressing charges...I have no idea. Yes, it is idiocy but I can't fight that right now, OK? I'm sorry. Listen, I don't know, just don't make it a fun thing for her to be out of school OK? I'm trying to get in touch with Jenna to see if she can come over right after school. You can go back to work as soon as she gets there. OK, I won't. Thank you so much...I really appreciate you."

"Hello, this is Marlene calling back. I just wanted you to know that someone is coming for Missy. No I can't get there right away, my friend Billy is going to...Yes, my friend...Well, that's why I'm calling you, so you know that it is OK with me to let him take Missy. No, I can't get there... a few minutes. Well, who do I have to talk to get approval for you to turn Missy over to him? I can't imagine this is the first time that someone has had to have a non-parent pick up their...How can I do that? If I could get you something in writing I could just pick her up. I can't get there...Can I talk to the principal then?...Well, look, I don't know what more to tell you. My friend Billy will there in a few minutes to pick up Missy. You have my permission to release her to him. If you don't want to do that, then you will just have to keep them both entertained until five o'clock or so."

"Chad, did you reschedule that meeting? You did? Can you change it back before anyone makes other plans? Well, I got someone else to...No Chad, I will be back in time...I will be...It doesn't matter Chad, why does that matter? I'm losing reception Chad, please just change the meeting back..."

"Oh, Jenna, thanks for calling back. Is there any chance you could come over right after school this afternoon. I had to get Missy out of school and I couldn't make it so Billy went to pick her up and I'm hoping you can relieve him so he can get back to work if he needs to. Sure. That's great. Thanks honey, you're a huge help."

"Chad, listen, I'm sorry to do this, but I need you to reschedule...I know what I asked you, but I'm stuck in traffic again, and I don't think I'm going to make it after all. Yes. Yes. No, I didn't. Look, Chad, I really don't have time to explain...OK, I mean *you* don't have time for me to explain the details; you just need to get the meeting rescheduled. Chad, I am beyond impressed at your encyclopedic knowledge of local road construction. It is truly one of the most astounding things I have ever experienced and I can't put into words how gratifying it is just to say I know you. Please reschedule the meeting for four o'clock. Bye."

"Hello, Principal Zimmerman...Yes...I know I sent him to get Missy. Is everything...Why would he...did you try to keep him...he said what? That doesn't sound like...Well, I'm sorry I'll try to figure out...That won't be necess...That's alright, I can do that. Yes. I will. Please let me find out what's going on before...OK, OK. Friday at two o'clock. Yes, I will. I will. OK. Good bye."

"Billy, did you get Missy? Is she OK? Did something hap...Yes, I know they're awful. What did they...? Yes, it's stupid. So what did you...? Oh great! That's just great! Of course, not...why would you concern...Alright, alright. We'll talk about it tonight. Is Jenna there? Are you going back to work? No, you go ahead. I'm going to try to make it to yoga....Does Missy need to talk to me? OK, tell her I love her; I should be back before seven. Ask her what she wants for dinner? OK. Bye."

In the entire history of the world, no one has ever wanted anything as much as Marlene wants a cigarette.

••••

The single story sprawling brick building, the extra wide bus loop at the front entrance, the cork bulletin boards, the immature looking room numbers, the knee level drinking fountains—all triggered memories; shudderingly uncomfortable memories. This was a world of playground bullies, of explanations dismissed and pleas ignored, of embarrassments and fears and narrow judgments. This was a child's first taste of helplessness in the face of ignorance empowered. This was the seed of all manipulation, envy and falsehood in the world. This was elementary school.

Insecurity. This was childish insecurity and Billy was really quite surprised at how strong an emotion it was in his forty year-old self. The fact remained, he had never come to terms with adults—he was on the cusp of middle age and instead of having grown to appreciate adulthood, he still resented it and those who had mastered it. He found himself thinking, "Wait until they try to pull any bullshit on me now."

He was about to enter The Office—the place where children are sent when they are bad. "Go to the office!" could stop a child's heart. He would have sworn it had the same smell of mimeograph ink and Lysol air freshener as the one in his elementary school. In 2nd grade he had been sent to The Office for some reason or other. Having never been there before he did exactly as he was told. He went to the office and sat quietly and unnoticed in the little waiting area. After a little over an hour his teacher appeared and was furious that he had not reported his transgression to the Principal. Billy's explanation that he didn't know that he was supposed to was taken as sarcasm and he was berated to the point of tears by his teacher who was joined about halfway through her tirade by the principal who had come out to see what was going on.

Billy still remembered sitting on the green plastic chair, looking up at two tall, severe, bespectacled women bearing down on him and the horrible feeling of being small and defenseless, unable even to beg for mercy. Now he looked over and saw Missy sitting in what could have been the exact same chair.

"You must be Billy," said the receptionist.

"Billy!" cried Missy and leapt almost directly from the chair into his arms.

"Missy stay seated!" barked a woman standing in an office doorway. Missy ignored her.

"Hi, sweetie! Are you OK?" asked Billy.

"Where's Mommy?"

"Mommy couldn't get out of work; I'm going to take you home OK?"

"Can we go play on the swings?"

"Sure, sweetie."

"You should know," said a severe, bespectacled woman emerging from an inner office, "that Melissa is suspended until we resolve her behavior."

"OK," Bill said with a smile; then to Missy, "Did you do something bad?"

Missy put on a poker face. Billy turned to the woman and could tell immediately that she was without a heart or a soul. The sign outside her office door said Principal. Billy sneered.

"She used language that we do not tolerate especially when directed at another student."

"I didn't think she knew any of the bad words." To Missy: "Did you use a bad word?"

Missy shook her head.

"Did you call someone a poopy-head?"

Missy shook her head.

"Did you call someone a pee-pee brain?"

Missy shook her head again and giggled a little.

"Did you call someone a toilet face?"

Missy laughed out loud and shook her head.

"You may think this a joke but we take such things quite seriously. This has become a legal issue." The atmosphere was thick with the Principal's hardened sanctimony.

"A legal issue? Maybe it's been so long since you were in school that you don't remember that kids call each other names all the time. That's just what they do. What sort of legal issue would it cause, a libel suit?"

"Melissa called another little girl a skank ho."

"Is she?" Billy deadpanned.

Missy smiled, shocked. The Principal flushed with indignation.

"I assure you this is not funny. We have a very strict policy on such—"

"It's a pretty stupid policy,"

"Those are the rules—"

"Do you really think she has any idea what she is saying?"

"We cannot make that judgment, our policy comes from the school board and it is quite clear. Such talk falls under the heading of Speech Intended to do Emotional Harm—"

"It's an insult. That's what kids do at that age. They insult each other. It doesn't cause emotional harm."

"It does indeed. Such behavior can be an indicator of hostile and even violent tendencies. We cannot risk that."

"So you're saying that the other little girl is completely traumatized and Missy is a potential mass murderer?"

"The school therapist will have to determine that after her examination. You should also know that the other girl's mother has many options for redress, both through the school and legal systems."

Billy seethed at the hopelessness of it. "C'mon Missy, let's get out of here. There's way too many skank ho's in this place."

Billy was furious, partly with the idiots in the school but mostly because he let his childish emotions make things worse. And he knew he had really, really made things worse. Why couldn't he have just picked up Missy and told them Marlene would be in touch?

He let Missy ride in the front seat next to him and play with the radio, then took her directly to the swings.

....

Yes...Missy is fine... There may have been a bit of a misunderstanding. Those people are awful...I've never heard anything so stupid...Well, the Principal may have misconstrued something I said as an insult...Listen, you know what, fu—forget them! I don't care what they think...Look, can we talk about it when you get home? Yeah, Jenna's here...No I don't think so. You want me to cut her loose? I was going to head over to my apartment and get another carload of stuff, but I can...No she's fine. You know how she is; she just shakes everything off after a few minutes. Missy! Your Mom says she loves you and what do you want for dinner?"

"Hooter's wings!" replied Missy enthusiastically.

"She doesn't care. Why don't I just pick up some Chinese on the way back?"

....

Marlene exchanged nods with Sarah at the beginning of class and raised friendly eyebrows to Ted, who she spotted in the back, then unrolled her mat and did some warm-up stretching. The lights went down, the new age music swelled, and Sarah led the class through a pre-planned set of contortions. There were the usual assortment of characters there—the groaners, the loud breathers, the first-time gigglers, the intense studies. Marlene found she was, with a bit of effort, able to keep the concerns of the day off her mind.

As she did in the final minutes of every class Sarah had them lie on their backs in near total darkness, with only the slightly echoing sound of Sarah sympathetic monotone stepping through all the major muscle groups and gently exhorting them to relax them completely, with the goal of achieving a stress-free state to be enjoyed for nearly a full three minutes.

"Thanks, Sarah."

Marlene found she said this in unison with a pretty young Asian girl. All three laughed.

Sarah said, "Midge, this is my friend Marlene. This is Midge, she's my latest star pupil."

"Very nice to meet you, Midge. Have you been a member here long?"

"Oh about a year or so."

"I was thinking it might be nice to have Midge along next time we all get together."

Marlene thought, "Yeah, that's just what we want, a twenty-year old hottie in the hot tub with us to make us feel so proud of our bodies." Marlene said, "Why sure, that'd be great. Of course, we only manage to get together once in a blue moon anymore."

"That sounds like it might be fun. It was nice meeting you. I'll see you later Sarah."

Marlene and Sarah exchanged smiles. "You would not believe the day I've had," Marlene sighed.

"I guess you must have needed this, it's been so long since I've seen you in class."

"I just can't keep up. I need to get a grip on things but I can't seem to do it."

They started to walk out. "So how are things going with Billy? Isn't he helping out?"

"Well actually he is. He was a big help getting Missy today." What followed was an overly brief and innocuous recap of the day as they slowly walked out of the yoga room, Sarah shutting off banks of lights as they went.

"Are you really planning on inviting your new little friend in the tub with us?"

Sarah laughed, "No, I don't think any of us want that. She's a sweet girl, I know she's young but I think you'd like her."

"Excuse me," said Ted who was just exiting the yoga room.

"Oh dear!" Marlene laughed. "Did we turn the lights out on you?"

Ted smiled, "That's OK, it was pretty funny."

"I'm sorry about that Ted," Sarah added sympathetically.

Still smiling, Ted said, "No harm done," and gave Sarah a gentle touch on the arm as he left.

••••

The remaining yoga endorphins drained from Marlene when Billy haltingly described his encounter with the elementary school authorities, as did the blood and spirit, leaving a cadaverous pallor. She dejectedly stared off into space as Billy vainly attempted to justify his behavior by describing the fathomless evil of the Principal and the hideous demons that must constitute the school board. Finally, Billy fell back into a chair and cried sincerely, "I fucked up. I know I fucked up. I'm sorry."

Marlene intoned vacantly, "Now I have to go up there and humble myself before those people to try to get Missy back into school. Not to mention show my face to all the other parents including our friend Dick, the educator."

"No you don't. They aren't worth it. Missy shouldn't be there, she should be in private school."

"Good God! How exactly am I supposed to afford private school?" snapped Marlene.

"Well, I could help you pay for it."

"You? You are going to help me pay for my daughter's private education? You just moved over five CDs, two pairs of jeans, a ceramic beer mug, and the *ESPN Baseball Encyclopedia*, and you are going to pay for my daughter to go to private school?"

In the next room Jenna asked Missy, "Did Billy really call Principal Zimmerman a skank ho?"

"Uh-huh! And then he called her a stupid toilet face! And then he said her face was like poopy!"

September 30

"We just need to be ready. That fat fuck goes out at night—probably to clean out the Little Debbie display at the Seven-Eleven—and when he does, we just need to be ready."

Billy stopped a passing clerk. "Excuse me, which aisle is breaking and entering?"

"Never mind him," Flip snapped. "Glass cutters?"

"Aisle twelve. There's a 20% discount if you apply for a Home Depot card."

"Thanks, we're just looking."

The clerk vanished.

"Quit foolin' around, wouldja?" Flip scolded out of the side of his mouth. "Whaddya want the whole town to know? Now all we need is Mr. 20% Discount to read about a burglary the police blotter and decide to rat you out, like a good citizen."

"Me?"

"You're the one who brought up breaking and entering."

"You think I'm taking the rap alone?"

"Hey. No snitching. We have to be clear on that. One of us gets fingered, he clams up. That's that."

"Fuck that. I get collared, I'll turn. I can't do time, man."

"I'm serious. We have to agree to clam up if we get caught."

"Fine, you just keep the smokes coming so I can bribe my way out of any ungentlemanly advances."

Flip grabbed a boxful of latex gloves, nodded wisely and tossed them into the cart. "Unless we get caught in the act I wouldn't worry about the cops. It's not like they're gonna send the forensics team in to get DNA samples. They'll only get wise if we try to fence the take."

"Christ. The take?"

"Yes. If we try sell any of the stuff we steal. That's how they catch perps."

"Oh my god. Perps?"

Flip regarded some double-sided tape with a knowing eye and lobbed it into the cart. "Duh. Perps. Perpetrators. Us."

"I know what perps means. I'm more worried about getting spotted in the act."

"You have black clothes, don't you? Of course you do. For clubbing. Dick, probably doesn't have a black cardigan, though. We'll stop at Target and get some ski-masks. And black overalls just to be safe."

"Wouldn't Halloween masks of presidents be more

appropriate?"

"No. Fuck. Ski-masks. Plain black. Keep it simple, stupid."

"Fine. What if we have to outrun an axe-wielding Otto?"

"We don't have to outrun Otto. We just have to outrun Dick."

••••

Removing the power cord to the television would have been a lot easier if her hands weren't shaking. Easier still if Missy hadn't been screeching bloody murder for the last ten minutes straight. Marlene placed the power cord on the highest shelf in the kitchen, along with her laptop and iPod. Missy could do nothing but rage against her now pre-technological existence.

As a planned effort to pre-exhaust Missy it was touch-and-go, and it was only at about the half-way point to the psychiatrist's office that Missy's lungs finally gave out. She slumped in her car seat like a spent wildebeest awaiting the inevitable crush of the lion's jaw.

"Mommy, why do I have to go?" she whimpered.

"Missy, I have told you this a hundred times. Your behavior is so terrible we need to find out if something is wrong with you."

"You think I'm crazy."

"I don't. But I need to know. And so does your teacher and your principal. I know I have never taught you to behave like this, have I? Did I ever tell you it was acceptable to be like this? Why do you think it's OK to be so defiant and—"

"What's defiant?"

"It's when you just do whatever you want, even when you are told not to. And screaming at your teacher. And refusing to get ready in the morning. And the name you called that other little girl—"

"Skank ho."

"Yes, Melissa, and don't you ever use that word again!"

Missy wept and sniffled profusely. "I'm sorry, Mommy. I'll be good. I promise. Please can we go home and watch TV now? I promise I'll be good."

"No we can't. It's too late for that now."

"I really promise."

"No, honey. No."

By the time they signed in and took seats in the waiting room, Missy was fully depleted and sat curled quietly in her Mommy's lap, Marlene gently stroking her hair. Both were flush from the radiant heat of emotional exhaustion.

The psychiatrist had a clinical, Germanic manner, as if he was newly arrived from a research stint at a Vienna sanitarium, yet Missy responded instantly to his utter lack of affectation and his professional deportment. He appeared to be unmoved by the fact that she was just a little girl. She was further disarmed, and quite impressed, by the forthright way he dealt with her mother: dismissively. It was a new and surprising adult mode of behavior. He did not refer to her in the third person or ask silly questions like what she wanted to be when she grew up or what she would like for her next birthday. The expectation was that she respond thoughtfully to direct questions. It was an odd but not disagreeable new experience.

"Melissa, you have been having trouble in school. Do you know why?"

"No."

"Well, then that's what we need to find out." This was said in the spirit of rolling up one's sleeves and getting to work with a positive attitude.

"Now, we know you have called another young woman a very bad name. Do you know what name we are talking about?"

"Skank ho."

"Where did you hear that name?"

"On TV."

"I try to keep my eye on what she wa—" Marlene started, but the doctor silenced her with eye darts.

"Do you know what it means?"

"Yes." Missy gleefully stood and hopped up on her chair. "It's a girl who goes like this!" She placed her hands on her hips, pouted her lower lip, and executed a perfect you-go-girl head jog.

"And why did you call the other young woman that

name?"

"Because when Tommy Margolis drew a stupid picture of her she did this." Missy repeated the mannerism.

"OK, Melissa. Please take your seat."

Missy sat quietly as the doctor allowed a longish moment to pass, simply regarding Missy while she sat composed and compliant, awaiting the next question.

"Do you dislike your teacher?"

"No."

"Do you like her?"

"Um, no."

"What about your classmates? Do you like them?"

"Some."

"You like them some, or you like some of them?"

Missy pondered. "I like some of them, but some of them I like some."

The doctor nodded. "And the young woman you called that name, do you like her?"

"Yes. She's like my third best friend. She likes to punch boys."

"Why does she punch boys?"

"She only punches the ones who don't know how to tie their shoes yet."

"I see." The doctor betrayed the barest of smiles.

"But she can't tell time very well, but I can."

"I see." Again, the doctor let a perceptibly over-long moment pass in silence. Missy just sat serenely.

"Melissa, tell me what you are learning about in school."

"Reading and science and history—"

"No, I mean tell the sorts of things you learn about."

"Global warming. We're going to be underwater soon because the ice caps are melting because of all the pollution. And the polar bears go instinct. And it's up to us to stop pollution."

"Do you do anything to stop pollution?"

"Um, I don't litter."

"I see. What other topics do you discuss?"

"Racism."

"Racism?"

"You shouldn't be racist because hating people is bad."

"Do you hate anybody, Melissa?"

"No. But in the old days people hated African-Americans for no reason. And they made Jews go into ovens that were like holograms. So we have civil rights."

"That's interesting, Melissa. Do you know what a Jew is?"

"A kind of person. And we are responsible for diversity so it doesn't happen here."

"I see. What else do you learn about?"

"I don't know. Oh, if a stranger touches you and your mommy isn't around you should scream for help as loud as you can. If somebody ever tried to touch me I would kick him and bite him until he let go and then I would run very fast and hide in a place only little kids could fit into."

The doctor allowed an even longer silence, this time

his look to Marlene was one of sympathy. Her eyes were thick with tears.

Before they got in the car to go home, Marlene held Missy in her arms more tightly than she ever had before.

••••

Few sights could have been more confidence inspiring to the other males in the room than seeing Dick positioned in an angular maneuver that marginally resembled Downward Dog. In their newly relative outlook they suddenly realized what truly awesome physical specimens they were, now of the same species—Homo Surburbanus Flexibilia —as the preternaturally limber instructor, or that dark, leggy, barely-legal Asian in the front; so far beyond the pathetic, lumpen, Neanderthal newbie.

For their part, the women saw all the men as undifferentiated and were oddly unaware that there was any anthropological hierarchy in evidence.

After the terminating Namaste, Sarah approached

Dick. "It's so good to see you here, Dick. I hope you enjoyed it—you look like you got a decent workout too," she said with a nod towards his sweat soaked white t-shirt.

"Oh, heh-heh, well it was...I guess I've slipped out of training a little, heh-heh."

"It's all about the journey."

"Yeah, is this the class Dora comes to?"

"Yes, well, she came just the one time."

Dick surveyed the room. His eyes landed briefly on Ted who offered raised eyebrows in recognition. "Well, I guess I better get going. Not good for us educators to be playing hooky, heh-heh."

Dick lumbered off and Midge took his place at Sarah's shoulder, wide-eyed and completing a phone conversation. She snapped the phone shut and cried, "That was the guy! Billy—the guy I told you about."

"Ooooh. So he finally called back, eh? What are you going to do?"

"I guess I'll go out with him."

Sarah flicked off the lights and took Midge's hand in

sisterhood. "He asked you out again?"

"Yeah. He said he wanted to meet for another drink. And I was like 'OK, I guess'. And he said we should meet for happy hour at Untapped Dishes. Day after tomorrow."

"Oh yeah? I haven't been there yet."

"Should I have said no? I mean—how long it took to call me. Maybe he just couldn't find anyone else—"

"What's the difference? Either you have a nice date or you don't. It's not the end of the world if you don't. Then at least you'll know."

"I guess."

"Call me and let me know how it goes, OK? Or maybe we can get lunch."

"Sure, let's do that."

Their sisterly grasp broke and Midge headed to the locker room. Sarah pulled her cell from her bag. "Hi Mar, it's Sarah. I was thinking it might be time to get together at that new spot we've been talking about— what's it called?—Untapped Dishes. Maybe a happy hour or something. Give me a call back. Bye."

Uncertain of her feelings, and half hoping it

wouldn't work out, she turned and started—almost colliding with Ted.

"You got me again," he said lightheartedly.

"Oh! I'm sorry, Ted. I had my mind on...I guess I'm just so used to seeing you in class now I don't even notice you."

"Next time I'll move to the front and scowl threateningly during warrior pose." He smiled and took a couple of steps away, then turned back. "Say, Sarah, would you possibly be interested in getting a cup of coffee sometime?"—Ha! She knew it! Of course that was it all along! Ha! He almost had her fooled with the whole Dora ruse—"I thought it might be nice to get to know ..."—Yes, of course. You like to get to know me a little better—"...a little more about your friends. And you. They seem like an interesting bunch."

Whoa now. That was awfully sincere. Was he really just trying to make friends? She tried to imagine his back story. A middle aged man on the hunt for a new circle of friends? For that, she felt a mild flash of empathy. Maybe he had divorced and his wife got all the friends. Ted, in cement. A rapidly aging man, surrounded all day by gruff construction rednecks pouring concrete. After some soul searching, he decides to take positive steps to change his life and expand his horizons rather than wallow in loneliness. He starts taking yoga. He fearlessly puts himself out there.

"Sure," she replied.

••••

Pammy felt a little like Dora's dimwitted sidekick as they sat across a desk from multiple architects in what had swiftly turned into a rapid fire q&a about the nature of the Rec Center project. Pammy had expected they were going to meekly approach this architectural firm in the guise of helpless, well-meaning housewives and ask naïve questions, eliciting carefully dumbed-down responses. Instead, Dora dove head first into a succinct explanation of the project, a description of the parcel of land, potential timetables, financing contingencies, and so on. The result was three very serious-looking and attentive professionals sitting across the desk, providing respectful and weighty answers. Dora must have spent some time pumping that Ted fellow for information. The thought of pumping a man for information impelled Pammy to consider which of the architects in current view she would choose to pump, including a critical consideration of their khaki-clad backsides. She finally settled on a tall, youngish, Latin-looking one working in a distant cube; her decision was affirmed when he rose to refill his coffee.

A subtle conflict was building between Dora, who was keen to get "accurate, non-binding estimates," and the cadre of architects who were exceptionally wary of putting any non-billable hours into a project that might bear no fruit. Finally, the architects acquiesced to a "brief, informal site visit" and "some very preliminary estimates" in the face of Dora emphasizing that it was a public project and that any unremunerated efforts would pay off by boosting their standing as "leaders in community involvement."

On the drive home Dora barely spoke to Pammy. She was immediately on her cell with Ted rehashing the meeting, then took a couple of shots at contacting Jenna, for no reason other than getting her to call back on principle. At this she failed, and at the point of dropping Pammy at home she reverted to weeping Dora.

"Thanks so much for coming with me. I was so intimidated."

"Oh, honey, you were amazing. You were like a force of nature. You didn't need me."

"I was?"

"Yes, you were. They didn't know what hit them."

"I don't know what I'm doing," Dora sniveled. "What do I do now?"

"Just what you planned, honey. Meet them at the site and hear what they have to say."

"Oh, I just feel like it's out of control. I'm in over my head."

"It's almost like being in love," Pammy sang.

Dora laughed at the thought.

••••

Jenna wished someone would invent a cell phone

that just didn't ring when certain people called. She had enough to worry about; Jimbo hadn't said ten words all day and she was too nervous for him to be nervous for herself. She snapped her phone off upon seeing her Mom on the caller ID. "Sorry about that."

Jimbo's younger sister, Binky, was an odd child, not the least reason being she didn't seem to mind the name Binky. She responded to none of the girlish cues Jenna expressed: the hair compliment, the slight giggle, the stupid-boy eye-roll comment. Just a bland, bespectacled little fireplug.

His father was friendly enough, though he left eye-contact to others. This was fine with Jenna, who wore her loosest shirt and most insulating bra in deference to the occasion, but it was obvious the visibility of her assets was not the problem. He was a deflector; all his replies were glib attempts at superficial humor, and all of them failed from Jenna's perspective.

Mother of Jimbo was evaluative in that way women are of other women, and was less hesitant to scan Jenna's form.

Dinner consisted of a substance similar in shape, color and consistency to Chicken Cacciatore, with sides of corn and oversized tater-tots. Binky ate with a certain sullen gusto, while her Mom kept a genial little chat going with Jenna. Jenna was doing pretty well, talking up her babysitting duties—identifying her as a girl responsible and respectable enough to be left with other people's children. After covering her parent's status in the educational community, which she spoke of in the blandest terms possible, the topic turned—as it always did—to Plans for the Future.

"We're trying to get Jim to focus on his college plans. You still need to fill out those applications."

"I know, Mom."

"I know you think it's OK to go to community college, but I at least want you to apply to Eastern."

"I know Mom, OK."

"Jenna have you applied anywhere?"

"Not yet. I'm supposed to meet with counselors to talk about picking a first and a fallback and a safety."

"I went to college based on where all my friends were going," interjected Jimbo's father, eyes on the far wall. "I wanted to have a readymade party crew so I didn't have to waste any time getting to know people." He grinned churlishly.

"Stop it," snapped Jimbo's Mom.

"Well, that's what college is all about."

"No, it isn't."

"My problem is I don't know what I want to study yet, so I don't know where to go," Jenna offered.

"We keep telling Jim he should major in engineering, being so good mechanically."

"Mom, I told you: that's not how engineering works. It's all math."

"Well you're good at math, too. You did well on your SAT."

"Problem is," Jimbo's father advised, speaking to his tater tots, "is there are no girls in engineering. Oh, sorry Jenna, I meant for looking not touching—"

Jenna smiled weakly, out of pity rather than anger.

Into the ensuing silence, Jimbo dropped a bomb. "I'm actually thinking of moving someplace else."

Even Jenna hadn't seen that one coming.

"Well, if you don't want to live at home, we understand. You can live in a dorm or—"

"No, I mean move away. Out of the area."

"You know your cousin is at Eastern, maybe he needs a roommate; you could share a place. Nobody's saying you have to live at home." Like all who are skilled in the art of not listening, Mother of Jimbo was responding to her inner narrative rather than external reality.

Jenna saw something approaching anger in Jimbo. Her instinct was to touch his hand gently but she resisted showing any sign of intimacy in front of his family.

"What does living at home have to do with anything? Did I say I didn't want to live at home?" Jimbo snapped.

"Well, I just assumed you intended—"

"Out of state tuition is very expensive, you know Jim," his father added, scanning the floor. "You don't want to get yourself in debt and have that hanging over your head when you graduate. It'll eat you alive, let me tell you."

"I can go part time. Or not go at all." Jimbo instantly realized he had violated perhaps the most terrifying taboo of all: not going to college. You brush your teeth before you go to bed, you always wear your seatbelt, and after high school you go to college. Case closed. It's just what you do if you are any sort of civilized person. He quickly added, "Until I establish residency."

Mother of Jimbo retook the reins. "Why? What is it you don't like here? Where—?"

"I don't know. Maybe Colorado. Or Seattle."

"But I don't understand why you need to go somewhere else. Why can't you do here what you are going to do there?"

"I don't know. Just to see what other places are like. Just to be somewhere else."

"Then go and see them. Why do you have to live there? What, do you expect us to fly you back across the country for the holidays? And you just abandon your little sister like that? You split up the family if you do that, you know. I don't understand why you have to do that. You didn't see you older brother leaving did you? He's perfectly happy to be nearby.

Why do you want to leave us?"

Jimbo just looked away and steamed. Everyone completed their meal in the eternal, excruciating two minutes of silence that followed.

"Can I help you with the dishes?" Jenna asked.

"No, I think we can manage."

Jimbo rose and placed a hand on Jenna's shoulder indicating it was time to leave.

"Thank you for having me over. It was a delicious meal."

Outside next to Jimbo's car they embraced tenderly.

"I'm sorry," they said softly in unison and exchanged smiles.

Jimbo said, "Why are you sorry? You didn't—"

"Shhh. I'll go with you. Wherever you want, I'll go with you."

Jimbo's shirt dampened with Jenna's tears.

••••

In spite of common opinion to the contrary, Flip had made significant strides in self-mastery since the onset of adolescence. He was now up to double digits in his string of days without flipping the bird to another driver and was quite optimistic about the possibility of keeping his middle digit holstered for a full fortnight, provided he could get through this fast food run with the damn kids and the damn wife driving him to desperate measures. One advantage to having the kids flopping and failing about in the back of the Grand Caravan was that his right arm was constantly reaching back and randomly slapping at them like a blind man trying to fend off an angry wasp. This, combined with the need to steer, fully occupied his hands, and acidic comments about the intelligence, judgment and ancestry of other drivers didn't count against his streak.

Whipping a quick left into the Taco Bell drive-thru, Flip shouted, "Hey! Hey! What do you want, tacos or burritos?"

One replied, "Taco! No, burrito! No, taco! No, burrito! No, taco—" devolving into maniacal laughter. A second suggested he "quit being so gay." The third declared with great hilarity that he'd rather eat boogers. This was also deemed gay.

"Just order four of each and we'll sort it out," Pammy sighed.

The incessant child noise finally reached a point where Pammy put a Tori Tornado DVD in the player and barked at the children to put on their headphones. This order was acceptable to them and they readily transformed into unblinking zombies fixated on the LCD screen in the back of the center armrest.

Flip hated that goddam DVD player. It cost extra because he saw no reason to upgrade to the Signature model on which it came standard and so was forced to shell out for it as an extra cost option of the lesser Premier model. He would have gladly paid a steep premium for any model that had ejector seats. Press a button and leave your passengers stunned at the side curb while you zoom off down the road to high adventure. Of course, high adventure rarely comes to those in minivans, and the ejector controls for so many seats would be too complicated. Flip needed something simple. Blaze westward in a '65 Mustang convertible. The picture of independent manliness, barreling around the mountains and through the canyons, stopping only for a beer and a meaningful conversation with the home-spun types at some ramshackle road house.

"Twelve-fifty," said the lazy-eyed teen at the drive-thru window.

Flip contorted to pull his wallet from his back pocket and handed the kid a twenty. He re-contorted to replace his wallet and added a torturous arch to his lumbar to get the change into his front pocket. In doing so, his foot slipped off the brake and the minivan lurched forward before he slammed it to a stop in semi-panic.

"What are you doing! Can you not wait until we get home to put the money away!" snapped Pammy.

Flip wrung himself back around to try to reach the drive-thru window to retrieve the bags of food and the five sodas from Lazy-eye, whose un-lazy-eye clearly emanated annoyance at having to adapt his stance to reach Flip's now mispositioned car. The driver behind had already pulled up to Flip's rear bumper and gave a honk and a wave indicating Flip should move along.

"Just a goddam second!" was Flip's polite reply.

Food retrieved, he pulled ahead and into a nearby parking space—an act Pammy disdained with savage contempt since they could just as easily eat while he drove. Dinner was distributed. The kids accepted the meal without averting their eyes. Then suddenly, without a whiff of warning, there was a singular and shocking occurrence. Without preamble, Flip said, "I'm thinking of getting a motorcycle."

Pammy half-laughed. "What?"

"I'm thinking of getting a motorcycle," Flip repeated with the quiet boldness of a defendant declaring his innocence in court.

"You don't know how to ride a motorcycle."

"I can learn. It can't be hard."

"You're not serious. You'll crack your skull open is what you'll do, you know how you are."

"What's that supposed to mean?"

"You do realize it's almost winter, don't you. Is this some kind of mid-life crisis?" Pammy smirked. "Did you order four burritos?"

Flip steaming from the response snapped, "Yes!"

"Well don't take it out on me. There's only three in the bag. Are you sure you ordered four?"

"Yes! Fuck! Yes! Gimme that!"

Flip snatched the bag and walked back to the drive-thru window. Excusing himself to the driver who was trying to pay, he turned to Lazy-eye and calmly inquired, "May I ask a quick question? How motherfucking hard is it to put a motherfucking burrito in a motherfucking bag?"

Lazy-eye stepped back in uncertainty.

The driver honked at Flip. "You can't walk up to this window. It's not for pedestrians."

"I'm not a pedestrian. That's my car over there. I'm returning to sort out my order." Turning back to still-stunned Lazy-eye, he pursued the topic, "Did you not understand me? Did I stutter? Do you need more detail? I ordered four burritos, there were only three in the bag. So again I ask, how motherfucking hard is it to put a motherfuckin—"

The driver honked again. "If you have a problem with your order you are supposed to go inside.

That's how it works. You go inside to correct your order. Haven't you ever done this before?"

Flip replied, "Sir, I understand your frustration. Let me explain: Fuck you." Turning once again to the window he was immediately handed a burrito in a bag and told, "We're very sorry," by someone in a tie.

The driver honked again and screamed, "You go inside to do this! You go inside! Inside!"

Flip reached into the drive-thru window and grabbed another bag of food. "Is this your order? Is this the one you've been waiting for?" He opened the bag, pulled out burrito and took a big bite of it. With a full mouth he said, "Now there is problem with your order. You can go inside to straighten it out."

Back in the minivan Flip handed Pammy the fourth burrito.

"Nice. Nice display for the kids," she commented.

"They haven't taken their eyes off that damn show."

"What's wrong with you?"

"Nothing. Nothing is wrong with me. What's wrong with you?" Flip choked down the last of his stolen bite of burrito.

"Normal people don't act like this!"

"Like what?"

"Like sneaking around in the middle of the night. Like having no regard for anything I ask of you. Like swatting the children constantly."

"I don't—"

"Yes you do. You're like a child. I have to constantly keep after you. How many times do I have to ask you to do something before you do it? You fight me on everything. Now it's a motorcycle—god knows where that came from! And you behave like a lunatic over a burrito!"

"I suppose you think I should have gone inside."

"I am not kidding around! You need to get grip on yourself. Normal people don't act this way."

Flip was oddly serene in his non-response. Finally Pammy added, "Normal men don't leave their wives untouched in bed for months at a time. You have a problem."

Flip sneered. He was insufficiently self-aware to see that he was very close to crossing a terrifying, life altering line into hating his wife. All that came out was, "There's nothing wrong with getting a motorcycle."

October 2

Sarah searched furiously for the proper state of consciousness, but no degree of effort or effortlessness would resign her to the anticipated dramatics. Even an attempt to affect a self-satisfied smirk only came out as a lunatic leer. This was not her. This was something out of a chick flick; vengeance through an eternal cliché. How could she have thought such an escapade would be in harmony with her spirit? It was the self-betrayal that was causing her distress.

No, that wasn't it. She was doing this for her friend, whose hopes and dreams were unknowingly at risk. How could she stand by and let Marlene get hurt like that? Helping her friends was true to her spirit.

Besides, it was just a prank, really. People pulled practical jokes on each other all the time. And, really, if anyone deserved to be taken down a peg it was Mr. Game Player himself. Let's see him talk his way out of this.

Sarah was amazed how someone like Marlene could be as blind as some love-silly schoolgirl. Marlene of all people; she was a resolute career woman; she had been through marriage, pregnancy, divorce, motherhood, yet still couldn't see straight. She should know.

She should know.

She should know what?

About men? About Billy? About what was good for her? Who was *she*?

Sarah pressed an involuntary hand to her stomach.

They stood in the lounge of Untapped Dishes waiting to be seated. Dora studied the menu like a heavyset woman with body issues, loneliness borne of a misguided divorce, and an ingrate of a teenage daughter. Marlene looked about with a habitual smile, the thinly masked tension of a late-thirties woman with a career, an insufferably bratty daughter, and a man-child lover.

They *should* know, shouldn't they? *They* should know. Maybe being spiritually healthy and clearsouled was not the key to fulfillment. What if self-possession and serenity didn't make you happier than a muddled karma and an endless battle with an unfaithful man? Maybe *they* do know.

Sarah found a seat, her head spinning. What had she done? From her impetus, they were about to walk into the dining room to the sight of Billy and Midge, quite possibly ruining lives out of...what? Concern for a friend? Nobility of purpose? How about arrogance? How about vindictiveness? Who was *she*?

"Maybe we should leave," Sarah muttered.

"Why? I'm sure it won't be long," Marlene offered.

"We're setting up your table right now," added the hostess.

Sarah flushed. "I'm not feeling too well. Maybe if we —"

"Well, hello!" cried Marlene.

Dora looked up and smiled in recognition, "I asked Ted to join us. I was beginning to think you weren't going to make it."

"I was early actually," Ted explained. "But I ran into

someone I know." He indicated the dining room with his thumb.

Marlene feared, correctly, that dinner conversation was now going to consist of endless exchanges between Dora and Ted about the rec center.

"Hi Sarah. Are you not feeling well?"

"No, I may not stay."

Ted replied with special certainty, "I'm sure you'll feel better once you get some food. I'm told this place is excellent."

"We have your table ready," announced the hostess, and without acknowledgment or even a glance to give her an out, everyone marched into the dining room, compelling Sarah to follow, hollow-eyed. She kept her eyes on the ornate ceramic floor tiles, then on the fine linen tablecloth as the busboy filled their water goblets. Thinking nothing but "Oh dear god," she raised her gaze to the olive oil bottle centerpiece, then around to the nearby tables. By the time the wine arrived she had scanned the entire restaurant. She laughed quietly.

"Sarah? Are you OK? Did you see something?" Ted asked.

"What? No. I'm just checking the place out. Is anyone else starving? I'm famished."

••••

Midge was, quite frankly, a little weirded out. She had heard of such behavior in the dating tales of her girlfriends over multi-hued martinis, but this was the first time she would have a story to add. There had to be a reason for the panicky rush to "get out of this joint" even before their drinks arrived. All sorts of possibilities ran through her mind as they drove across town to a "much better spot." "I like this place, have you ever been here?" he had asked.

"Nope, never." It was darker and quieter. Maybe it was closer to where he lived—and his bedroom. Maybe he just liked it; he seemed to know the bartender. Maybe he was going to give him a signal to drug her drink so he could molest her.

After a self-conscious moment of silence, Billy said sheepishly, "There was someone back there I didn't want to see."

Midge said nothing, wiser than her years.

"I should have told you before we left, but I felt like a complete goober trying to hide from someone like a scared child."

Midge just raised a sympathetic eyebrow. "A goober, eh?"

"Anyway. If you still want to go there, I'll take you another time."

She smiled. "Sure. But they might want a security deposit before they take our order."

He laughed. Again he thought of her as terrific, and this time he told her.

"Are you sure you're not trying to make me think you're some kind of mystery man—attract me with your dark intrigues?"

"No, no. Not that. Not at all. Is it working?"

"I don't know yet. I suppose the goober you were talking to in front of the men's room was your CIA contact?"

"Ha." Billy got sincere. "He alerted me that a woman I know was about to show up."

"Oooh, a 'woman you know.'"

"It would have been awkward to be seen with you."

"So, not your mom?"

"Not exactly." This was it. This was his opportunity to come clean; to be honest and end the ridiculous charade before it got out of hand. If he let this thing continue they would build up a store of shared experiences and intimacies, at which point a split would be emotionally expensive. She would be hurt or shamed, probably both if he couldn't manipulate her into dumping him. If she ended up the dumpee she might turn to chocolate and get all fat and depressed. She didn't deserve that. But right now, right this instant, it was cheap and easy. Do it now.

"It was someone I was involved with." Technically true, he omitted that he still was involved with her, deciding omission was a good compromise between ignominious honesty and outright falsehood.

"Ah. And I'm sure she still has hopes of getting you back."

"I don't know. It would have been uncomfortable in any case." What in God's name was he doing?

Conversation continued, slouching towards more innocuous subjects, lacking the erotic charge of their previous meeting. In time, the topic defaulted to comparative pop culture and Midge made the sympathetic comment: "I'm sure you feel about my kid stuff the way I feel about Tori Tornado or something."

Billy thought of Missy. "What is the deal with that? Every kid I know is insane for it."

"Do you have kids?"

"Me, no. No. I have a sort-of niece. She would do anything for one of those dolls. Even the boy kids want it. It's a doll. What in the world does a child want with doll these days, especially boys? Don't all they do is play video games anymore?"

"Tori Tornado is much more than doll. It's a way of life. See, you jack your doll into your USB port and you're hooked into the whole social network. You get episodes downloaded in advance of TV. You get puzzles and games. You get to create an identity for yourself. You swarm on key gear. You—"

"Huh?"

"Swarm on gear. Tori recommends certain products and her minions do what's called swarming. They all rush to order them online until they're out of stock. It's called swarming. It could be anything—shoes, backpacks, toys, whatever—but the more crap you can buy before it's gone, the more status points you have, and the earlier you get the advanced episodes and games and such. Plus, bragging rights for your online network identity. Some parents have actually complained to the FCC, or wherever, when their kids are traumatized by not swarming in time. It's incredible."

"The whole thing is a marketing ploy? To sell junk to kids?"

"Yeah."

"It's genius."

"Yuh. Evil genius."

"But still." Billy could easily see himself going broke making sure that Missy had more status points than everyone else in the neighborhood. Hell, he'd probably hack her password and stay up nights monitoring Tori for new swarms just so she wouldn't miss out on any out-of-their-time-zone crap.

So, yes. The answer was yes. He would help pay for Missy to go to private school. Seriously, now, it was time to permanently wrap this up with Midge.

He was about to. Or at least he thought he was probably about to as he walked Midge to her door. Then she turned and kissed him. A sultry, open-mouthed kiss; soft and wet and smoldering. She withdrew, her hands coming to rest steadily on his chest.

"I..." Billy was swamped by guilt and lust. Her skin had the flawless gloss of a perfect pearl. He rested his hands on her hips, half pushing, half pulling. She angled her hips forward and smiled cautiously. Her plush hair was delicately jostled, random strands temptingly dangling, aching to be brushed gently aside to fully reveal her vulnerable eyes. He took her head softly in his palms and pulled her lips to his, deeper and more intensely than the first kiss. When he opened his eyes she was looking up at him like a like a freshly ripened child. He stepped back.

"I...this is a little fast for me."

"Um, OK," came her uncertain response.

"I guess it's my turn to be nervous."

She closed ranks and asked, "What are you nervous about?"

That rarest of things, a second chance, was now staring Billy in the face. The correct answer was "Look, I'm sorry to have led you on like this, because I really like you and I'm—obviously—very attracted to you, but I'm kind of involved with someone else and I don't think it would be fair to go any further." He knew it was right. He knew it. Her eyes were shining a deep lacquer black. His hands could nearly fit completely around her waist.

"Look, I'm sorry to have led you on like this but... I'm trying not to rush into things anymore. I guess I'm old fashioned. I mean, I've done that all my life and it hasn't gotten me anywhere. Well, actually, I think it's gotten me a lot of pain mostly, and I'm too old not to learn from my mistakes anymore." Mealy-mouthed coward.

"Oh, OK."

Things cooled off quickly.

"I'm sorry if you're disappointed. But we don't have

to be in any hurry, do we?" Spineless wimp.

Midge was thoroughly confused by the whole evening. Her thoughts jumped about: was he having some kind of a mid-life crisis, because it sounded like something someone would say if... the whole wishy-washy thing was not what she expected from...is he in the middle of some sort of emotional...he seemed like the kind of guy who knew what he wanted but... "I suppose we don't."

Billy said, "I'll call you. Let me make it up to you." Lying, cheating, piece of shit.

She was not convinced she wanted him to. "Sure. No problem."

••••

With her nearly virgin New Balance walking shoes still sparkling white, Dora returned home from an exploratory mall-walking session. As exercise it was fine but the other walkers, though polite, were quick with a cliquey glare and some were quite snippy if they were spoken to with their earbuds in. Obviously, there were dues of submission to pay if she wanted to fit in. She recycled the plastic bottle of her sports drink, happy to read that it was only 100 calories per serving, blissfully missing that the bottle contained two and a half servings.

The pink envelope that had been slipped under the door stood out so starkly in the preternaturally neat room that is may as well have been a turd.

Dora opened the note. She read it through, quivered slightly, and looked to the ceiling. She read it again, swallowed audibly, then crumbled to her knees and wept from the depths of her soul.

....

The specter of sex hovered over Billy. Through everything he did and thought, his failure of will was sending out tendrils like a creature from the deep, undermining his confidence, stifling his enthusiasm, worrying him like a schoolyard bully. A man would not have passed up a night with Midge, except out of deep conviction. But if he had such conviction, how did he get himself in a position where he had to make another call to her?

Was he deluding himself that moral conviction was the cause, when in fact he was intimidated by her youth? Billy knew the inevitable destination of this line of thinking was the ultimate reality: Mortality. Not exactly a confidence builder. Jesus, it was just a date! He should have bagged her—notched his bedpost in robust masculinity; he would have been only slightly more of dirtbag than he was now, but at least he would have felt like a man. Now all he could do was snap at Marlene for no damn reason like some yippy little Chihuahua.

"Billy!" Marlene called.

"What!"

"Do you have any—"

...virility left? ...sex drive at all? ...balls? "Any what?"

"Any preference for a movie? Is that OK to ask?"

The doorbell rang and Skippy the beagle nearly went apoplectic with snappy howls of warning.

"Skippy shut the...! Be quiet! Shut your yap! Christ!"

"Mom, Billy's swearing again!" laughed Missy.

Billy opened the door. It was Jimbo.

••••

Really, he wasn't bad looking. Not her type at all, but at least he didn't do the comb-over thing. And his clothes, though utterly devoid of anything resembling color, were nicely pressed. He was so forthright, even aggressive, in suggesting they get a nightcap at the bar that the others made quick excuses about having to get home. Yeah, he looked transparently conventional, but that's not bad. Well groomed. But could there be more underneath? She would see how he stood up.

"Are you a Christian?" Sarah asked with intentional impertinence.

Ted produced a slightly absurd smile. "Not so much. I'm half a Jew ethnically, but I'm not very religious in the usual sense." He waited with quiet bemusement for the next interview question.

"Are you a Republican?"

"Don't really have strong political affiliations."

"Who did you vote for?"

"Who should I have voted for?"

"Bad answer."

"Oh, why is that?"

"It means you're a Republican. Only Republicans are afraid to say they're Republicans."

"Why would they be afraid?"

"Because they know people won't like them."

"Oh. So you don't like Republicans?"

"I disagree with them."

"Do you dislike everyone you disagree with."

"No."

"So then it's other Democrats who don't like Republicans?"

"Yeah."

"But not you."

"Yeah."

"That's pretty shallow of them. I mean, if you're right and I'm a Republican, I just found out you are a Democrat, yet I like you. Apparently I couldn't expect the same courtesy from most Democrats in return. Doesn't that make you ashamed to be a Democrat?"

"No. I mean, I never said I was a Democrat."

"Oh. Well that's good; I'd hate to think you were associated with such an intolerant organization."

"Clever."

"Clearly I'm dazzling you."

"How about the environment?"

"How about it?"

"How do you feel about global warming?"

"I'm against it, but less so in the winter. This is a fascinating series of questions. Usually, I get questions about my personal history, my taste in movies, my hobbies..."

"It's more important to know where you stand on the big things. You don't seem to have many strongly held opinions."

Ted gave her piercing look that she wouldn't have expected from such a round face. "So you have history with Billy."

"Nnn...uh, what? Why do you say that?"

"Because of how you set him up earlier," Ted stated flatly, maintaining steady eye contact.

"What are you talking about?"

"You were talking to that girl Midge about a certain restaurant after class, when you turned the lights off on me. Then Dora calls me and says you are setting up a dinner with her and Marlene and would I like to come, it just happened to be that same restaurant. Then I get here early and there's Billy only he's not with Marlene, he's at a cozy table for two with—"

"OK. All right."

"Sorry, if I disrupted your plans."

"I made a mistake, OK? Did you tell Billy?"

"I just innocently mentioned that everyone was meeting there shortly. He got the hint and left."

"Thanks for that."

Ted maneuvered his expression to one of solemn sympathy.

Sarah continued, "Look, that wasn't me, ok? I don't know why...It goes against everything I try to believe...Yes, Billy and I were involved but that was a long time ago and I just...I didn't want to see Marlene suffer."

"Ah. So he cheated on you?"

"No. I mean not technically. He was just...I don't know...he was just never all in. He was always about himself at the core. I mean, he said the right things and did the right things, but it wasn't...I don't know...genuine. I mean, it's OK now; he was never the one for me. We were always very different; different values, different paths. So I knew it wasn't going to work. He just...I don't know...he just should have given more."

Ted was silent, encouraging her to continue.

"Look, I'm ashamed I did it, OK. Let's just move on."

"You should perform some penance to cleanse your soul."

"Cleanse my soul?" she asked incredulously.

"Yeah, cleanse your soul. It's obviously eating at you. Deception will do that if you're not cut out for it."

"You mean something like confess? Are you a

Catholic? To who? Billy? Midge?"

"No, that's more like the razing the land and salting the earth. Why don't you just use your matronly influence with Midge to convince her to end it with Billy? Bottle of Pinot Noir OK?"

Sarah nodded, dumbstruck. He nailed it. That was exactly what she needed to do. That Ted, the balding, Baptist-looking, khaki-wearing, possible Republican, could have such insight and depth sent her reeling. It would be many weeks until she gave a second thought about his appearance again.

Had he been present, Billy would have been equally awestruck that Ted in Cement had such astounding game.

••••

But at the moment, Billy was driving Jimbo to meet Jenna. Jimbo told Billy that his car was broken down and he needed a ride to meet up with Jenna and "some friends." The lie was obvious and Jimbo knew it, so Billy rightly assumed he was being handed plausible deniability. Jimbo directed them into a bright and friendly looking Starbucks anchoring a generic-looking strip mall. Billy parked immediately next to Jimbo's Volkswagen and gave it an obvious look of evaluation which elicited no comment from Jimbo except, "Come on in for a minute, we need to talk to you."

Inside was an impatiently waiting Jenna, holding a small chai latte in both hands and clad in a bright blue t-shirt that said *Visual Aid*. Billy could only sigh.

"You want a coffee or something?" Jimbo asked, offering a chair.

"No, I'm fine," replied Billy, taking it.

Extended silence followed. Billy raised his eyebrows in encouraging enquiry. He had to hold them up for a few seconds before Jenna exasperated, "We need to borrow some money."

Billy's eyebrows plunged. "You're pregnant?"

"Gawd no!" cried Jenna.

"But it's not really a car problem," he responded to Jimbo.

"We're going away, to be together," Jenna said. "We

just need some money to hold us over until we get set up. We'll pay you back."

"Absolutely, I promise we will," added Jimbo.

Great. How was he supposed to play this one? The standard adult response would be, "Where are you going? Do your parents know? You can't support yourself! You have to finish school! You don't know what you're doing!" Anything along those lines would amount to instant shutdown and just reinforce their desires. Instead Billy asked, "How much do you need?"

"Just a couple hundred. Whatever you can spare," replied Jimbo

"Can you get us five hundred?" Jenna asked immediately.

"How much do you have already?"

"I have—we have a little over eight hundred," Jenna said.

Billy pulled out his wallet and removed an indeterminate amount of bills. He paused mid-action as if distracted by thought and said, "Wait—I have to know your plans."

"Can't you just trust us?" Jenna pleaded.

"The less you know, the better," added Jimbo.

"Look, I'm sure you have a good plan, but I can't just hand over money to you. You realize that makes me culpable for anything you do. Aiding and abetting. Aiding and abetting *minors*."

"Oh my god," cried Jenna. "What, do think we're going off to score crystal meth or something?"

"No. But whatever it is I am now officially the adult supervision, so I'm on the hook for it. I've got to know."

"We're going to—" Jimbo started.

"Promise you won't tell my father," Jenna interrupted.

"Promise you won't tell anyone," Jimbo concurred.

Billy considered for a brief moment to be sure he was OK with breaking the promise if necessary. "All right. Now tell me."

"We're going to Seattle. Tonight. Driving straight through. We'll get there day after tomorrow." Jimbo explained.

"Then what?"

"Then I'll find a job," Jimbo said, showing him printouts of Craigslist ads for mechanics.

"We'll both get jobs," Jenna said.

"Where will you sleep?"

"We'll get a cheap motel room until we get jobs, then we'll get a place," stated Jimbo showing him Google Maps of motel locations in and around Seattle.

"Who fucking cares where we sleep! We'll sleep in the car if we have to!" Jenna snapped.

Billy folded his arms. "You can't rent an apartment, get a job, or check into a motel room without proving your age."

"We have fake IDs."

"Of course you do."

Billy stared deeply and sullenly at the two of them. He saw the desperate adolescent hostility behind Jenna's moist pout. He saw the desperate adolescent insecurity behind Jimbo's hesitant chin. He tried to imagine their future. In all likelihood, they'd have so much trouble getting away with using their fake IDs they'd give up and have to make the soul-crushing call back home for help.

And even if they did get settled in, it would be some kind of rat-bag dump, probably student housing near some university. They'd be living pretty much right on top of each other; their cell phone subscriptions would expire; they'd be without cable TV and Playstation for the first time in their sentient lives.

And even if they managed to put up with each other and the insufferable boredom, what would come next? The GEDs, then the stress of night school at community college while holding down demeaning jobs, then the maddening effort to kick their careers into gear to get some semblance of financial security, or even more stressful and divisive, start a business of their own. They had no idea.

And even if they managed to reach entry-level middle class, then followed children and suburban mortgages and other minefields that Billy hadn't firsthand knowledge of, but they must be far beyond any previous challenge.

And even if they made it that far, Jimbo's instinctive agreeability and reticence would incite a simmering contempt in Jenna, while Jenna's dominance and self-regard would stir a smoldering resentment in Jimbo. Something was sure to snap. They would probably end up either cynically divorced with a troubled child or two, or trapped in the web of a wrenchingly dysfunctional marriage.

That was about the best they could hope for. It was insane. Totally insane.

Billy handed them the three hundred dollars he had in his wallet and said, "Come with me."

They exchanged anxious glances and followed him to an ATM just outside. He withdrew another four-hundred and handed it to them. Then he grabbed them both firmly by the arm and looked at them with his own worn and weary version of adolescent desperation. "Listen to me. I need your word on some things before I let you go. First, you'll both contact your parents regularly to let them know you're OK. I don't care if you tell them where you are or not, but you have to let them know you're OK. That's bigger and more important than your crazy plan to get out of here, you understand me? I will not let them suffer not knowing. If I find out your parents haven't heard from you by tomorrow night I will spill the beans and I'll personally hire every private eye and bounty hunter west of the Mississippi to find you and drag your asses back. Got it? Promise me."

"OK, we will."

"The other thing is you never, ever, EVER tell anyone where you got this money. Not your friends, not your family, not even your fucking diary, understand? You. Take. This. To. Your. Grave."

Jenna leapt up and kissed and hugged Billy with tears in her eyes.

"OK, we will. And we'll pay you back. You'll see."

Billy patted Jimbo on the back. "Yeah, OK. Whatever. Call your parents tomorrow night."

••••

"This is insane," Billy declared.

Flip and Dick were standing in the driveway, arms folded across their chests, staring dead-eyed as if they were mobbed-up debt collectors. Billy would have been intimidated by their deportment had he not known them better. As he exited his Audi, Flip tossed him a set of black overalls and a ski mask, quietly announcing, "It's time."

"Where are we going?" Billy asked following behind them like a confused child.

"My house," said Dick. "Jenna's not home. Out with Jimbo."

"Oh," Billy mumbled.

They stood in Dick's living room, lights out, speaking in golf announcer whispers.

"This is insane," observed Billy once again, while hurriedly pulling on his coveralls.

"Listen. He'll be leaving shortly. He goes out between 10 and 10:15 every Friday and is gone for at least 45 minutes..." Flip hissed.

"Probably looking for some blood to suck," spat Dick.

"...so that should give us plenty of time. We'll go around to the back door. His house backs up to the trees so we won't be seen. We can jimmy the screen door then cut the glass on the main door and open it from the inside."

Dick's cell phone caused everyone to jump.

"Damn it, Dick! Turn that off! Billy, turn yours off too. The last thing we need is to be in a tight spot and have a phone go off."

"It's Dora. I should probably take it."

Flip swiped it from his hand and snapped it off. "No! Jesus, you guys need to take this seriously! This isn't a college prank, this could go bad."

Billy sheepishly shut off his cell.

Flip added, "Besides Dick, why are you still at her beck and call? Shouldn't she be calling Ned if she has a problem."

"Ted," correctly Billy, adding, "and you're being an ass."

Dick was just staring at Flip. He snatched his cell back from Flip and pocketed it. "Oh and one more thing Flip: Fuck you. You are an ass."

"This is just now occurring to you guys?" Flip replied. "Come on, let's go wait out back. As soon as he pulls out we'll follow the hedgerows behind the houses to the end of the block then haul ass across to his backyard. We should only be under the street lights for a few seconds."

....

"Well, Flip's AWOL again." Pammy was marching down the street toward Marlene's house, having checked to see that Flip's car was still in the garage.

"Billy too," Marlene replied. "He went out a while ago but his car is back." She left her porch and marched off to intersect with Pammy.

"Good for nothing."

"Something is going on. Billy left without saying a word. Then he's back without saying a word. Now he's out again."

"You haven't heard a motorcycle have you? Flip threatened to buy a motorcycle the other day. Can you imagine?"

"There are no lights on in Dick's house either."

"What could they possibly be doing together?"

"They're completely different,"

"Dick, god only knows. Flip I could see out buying a motorcycle just to spite me. Billy out chasing... It'll just sit in the garage. He'd never ride it."

Now face to face in the fountainless cul-de-sac, they both flipped their cells closed. Pammy squinted and swiveled her head to scan the street.

"Out chasing what?" asked Marlene firmly.

"What? Oh, I don't know. I'm just talking."

"Do you know something you're not telling me?"

"I just mean that it's unlikely they would want to do the same things. I mean, Billy has, well, he's always been...he's always had a wandering eye. Flip hasn't been...that sort...for years, he wouldn't know how to approach a—"

"A motorcycle?" Marlene folded her arms.

Jawlines went taut. Lips went thin. Tones went sardonic.

"Well, I think you see what I mean. Say do you suppose they are all at Billy's condo? He still has that, doesn't he?"

"Yes that's possible. I imagine Flip hasn't been off

the leash in years, he probably leapt at the chance."

"Ha! I bet they're watching porn. I'm sure Billy needs a bit of that sort of warmth and affection now and then."

"That's probably it. I hope Flip doesn't get confused at the lack of cellulite."

They stood eye to eye. Seething. Hostile. Coiled to strike. Women with bared claws and venomous fangs. Women neglected. Women deprived of primal sexual influence. Women shamed by the impotence of their femininity. Women reduced to little more than men. Would that they could growl and bellow, beat their chests and throw haymakers. Instead what followed was five solid minutes of shrill, raging rebuke laced with affronts and slurs including a "shriveled-up hag", a "saggy old barge", a "dried-up wench", a "flabby ball-buster", a whopping seventeen "bitches" including "fat" and "frigid" modifiers, and a terminating "insufferable twat."

••••

From a second story window Missy watched the

battle in curiosity. "Uh oh. Somebody's going to have to see the doctor for an evaluation," she said to herself out loud, dancing about to some sing-songy lyrics that she thoughtlessly recited. Resuming her position in front of the window she began jumping up and down because she needed to go to the bathroom, but then she spotted another fascinating sight. "Evil villains," she said, again out loud. She knew exactly what to do. From the time she was barely sentient, a parade of authority figures of every stripe had earnestly drilled into her what to do in emergencies—if you're lost, if a stranger approaches you, if somebody you're with falls ill, and of course, if you see a crime in progress. Without a moment's hesitation she placed the call.

"911 emergency response," came the prompt answer.

"There's some bad men going into Otto's house."

"Uh wha? Would you repeat that?"

"There's some bad men going into Otto's house."

"What's your name, sweetie?"

"Melissa."

"How old are you, Melissa?"

"Six."

"Is one of your parents home?"

"My mommy's outside having a fight with Pammy."

"A fight? Do they have weapons—guns, knives?

"No."

"What's the fight about?"

"I don't know. Maybe boob jobs."

"Are you scared, Melissa? Do you feel like you're in danger?"

"No. But I have to go potty."

"Do you know Otto's address?"

"No, he lives on the other end of the street. He's got a big tummy."

"And you saw bad men going into his house?"

"Yeah, and they had masks over their faces."

"OK, Melissa, can you get your Mom—"

"I have to go potty now. Bye-bye." Melissa hung up

to go potty and forgot having made the call by the time she was done.

The 911 operator instantly checked Melissa's address through caller ID and also determined that there was an Otto who lived close by. After some efficient discussion with the dispatcher, a mildly annoyed uniformed officer was routed to the scene.

····

Flip tried to slide a credit card through the gap in the door jam, but the only result was a snapped American Express. He retrieved the glass cutter from the black duffle bag and etched a perfect semi circle in the corner of the door window and taking a small wrench handle attempted to knock out a corner of the pane with increasingly forceful blows until the entire window shattered. "We're in," he announced as he reached through and unlocked the door.

"We can't really be doing this," Billy observed.

"We'll make this fast. Follow me through the kitchen, then right to the basement."

They pulled off their masks and Dick brandished a can of spray paint and started shaking it.

"You have got to be fucking kidding me," Billy said as they moved into the kitchen.

"He needs to know this isn't an ordinary robbery. That's the point, isn't it? This is blow for justice," Dick replied.

"No. Stop. Right there." Billy snapped. "This is ridiculous. It's nothing more than a practical joke."

"Oh look," replied Flip with his head in the refrigerator. "Who wants some cold pizza?" He opened a box and stuffed a slice in his mouth before offering it around. Dick took one.

Billy said, "That's good. That makes sense, because you are both out to fucking lunch."

"Oh what now?" asked Flip as he led them onwards. "Does the man-child want to be an adult all of a sudden?"

Dick sniggered, delighted that Flip was picking on someone else.

"Fuck you, Flip. And fuck you too Dick. 'Cause you're both so fucking happy in your fucking marriages."

"I'm not in my marriage any more. So fuck you," Dick corrected.

"Uh huh," smirked Flip as they marched down the basement stairs. "Someone else is in there now."

"Fuck you, Flip," Dick repeated.

"At least my nads don't function solely as chew toys," Billy added.

"And fuck you, Billy. You've never even taken a shot at marriage. What do you know about nads?" Dick snapped.

"I've never had a nine-iron rammed up my ass either. Guess I'm missing out."

"Everybody here who has a functioning marriage say 'fuck you,'" suggested Flip. "Fuck you."

"Everybody here who understands the meaning of the word 'functioning' say 'fuck you,'" replied Dick. "Fuck you."

"Fuck me," exclaimed Billy as he turned on the light.

They stood mesmerized in the center of Otto's basement, surrounded by towering, magnificent mountains of pure stuff. Piles of iPods in various colors; four vintage Bang and Olufsen turntables; a dozen or so cell phones of a species that Billy didn't recognize, with Korean-language packaging; two pairs of what appeared to be original Air Jordans still in their boxes; a wall full of CDs and game cartridges, comic books and pulp paperbacks stored in thick plastic wrappings, shelf after shelf of figurines—Lladro, Precious Moments, and such; baseball caps; movie posters; ancient computers; an Underwood typewriter; watches locked in a glass top case; a beaten up Evinrude outboard motor; half a dozen well-worn Gibson guitars.

And a score of Tori Tornado dolls.

"Yes! Uh-huh! I knew it! I knew it!" cried Dick. "Goddamn corrupt fascist!" He removed the can of spray paint from his jacket.

"Dick," admonished Billy to no purpose. Dick started to spray paint the one bare wall in the basement.

"Hello Mary Jane!" called Flip. He lifted an oversized plastic bag filled with something that wasn't oregano. "I guess this explains the Twinkie addiction."

"Unbelievable! Look at all this!" Billy began look

more closely through the piles of merchandise, punctuating his investigation with occasional "Wows!" and "Holy shits!"

"Billy, is comeuppance spelled -ance or -ence?" asked Dick.

"-ance," answered Billy.

"Don't you know? You're the educator," snarked Flip.

"Fuck you, Flip. I thought I made that clear," snapped Dick, obviously in a fighting mood.

"Now now, Dick," consoled Flip. "Why are you wasting time with that spray paint? You want him to suffer..." Flip turned and waved a big ol' honkin' extra large spliff at them, "...why not make use of his ganja?"

"Oh for fuck's sake," cried Billy.

Flip waived the joint with beaming pride. "Not bad, eh? I haven't rolled one of these in twenty years. Just like riding a bicycle."

Flip fired it up and took a long, laughing drag. He then exchanged it for Dick's spray paint. Dick took his hit, holding his breath like a champ.

"This is insane," Billy said mechanically.

Dick coughed out his hit and waived the joint at Billy who took his turn.

The years since college had worn away their resistance and in a few short minutes they were borderline giddy as they worked it down to the roach.

"Here's to 'Greedy money-grubbing cheaters getting their comeuppance!'" Flip decreed, verbalizing Dick's graffiti. He then took the spray paint and added, 'Oh, and dude, thanks for the weed,' which was deemed the single funniest thing in the history of all time. Then, just as they were entreating Flip to roll a follow-up, they heard a knock at the door.

"Police officer!"

They froze, unsure if they heard what they heard.

Another aggressive knock. "Police!"

They frantically ricocheted about, crying "Oh, shit!" in muffled whispers. Flip tossed the spent joint aside. Dick began vigorously wiping the fingerprints off the can of spray paint. Billy said, "Godammit, I told you this was insane," grabbed a Tori Tornado doll, and darted up the stairs. Dick immediately fell in behind him. Flip managed to grab an armful of the dolls before following.

Billy stopped at the back door for a cop check. Another knock came, and yet another, "Police officer!" clearly from the front of the house. They flew out the back door and through the hedgerows behind Otto's yard. Flip tripped over god knows what in the dark, jamming his big toe and crying, "Goddam son of a bitch!" Billy snapped, "Shut up!" Dick called, "Sic Semper Tyrannis!" Billy snapped, "Shut up!" They kept running, coming in behind Marlene's house around by the garage entrance. They yanked open the side door and pulled up to a sudden stop, their jaws at their knees.

Equally shocked, Marlene stood facing them. Completely naked. A cigarette held gracefully between the index and middle finger of her right hand.

The entirety of creation entered a phase of paralyzing inscrutability for about seven seconds. Nobody even thought to breathe. Then Flip said, "Whoa," and creation rebooted. Marlene cried out in shock, instantly positioned her arms for maximum coverage, and kicked the door shut.

The men exchanged uncertain glances. Billy barked, "Well, get out of here!" and bolted into the garage himself.

There, an immeasurably flustered Marlene was trying to re-dress. Billy stopped her. She looked up at him and started to speak. Billy kissed her. She started to apologize for having cigarette breath, but Billy kissed her again. He put one hand over her throat and with the other pulled off the few shreds of clothing she had managed to put back on. Forcefully turning her back to him, in full view of Tori Tornado, he bent her over the hood of his Audi.

••••

Flip and Dick slunk wordlessly down the street, both too scared to glance back at Otto's house. When they reached Flip's driveway they stopped and looked at each other. Flip shrugged. Dick shrugged. Flip went inside.

Pammy was marginally hysterical as usual, although the standard admonitions to the children were tinged with a certain sorrowful, self-pitying tone and the endemic hostility in her eyes was supplanted by a wan puffiness. Flip stood poised majestically the doorway until they all looked up at him and only then, with a flourish, did he gently lob a Tori Tornado doll to each child.

The subsequent moment of silence was the first the household had experienced in several years. And it didn't end abruptly. With quiet intensity the children unpackaged their bounty and gathered around the laptop.

Tears welled up in Pammy's eyes. She wrapped her arms around Flip and buried her head in his chest. She looked up at him as he held her in tender confusion. "You know you're still my big hero, don't you?" They kissed deeply. With the children completely involved in jacking-in and swarming, Pammy nodded towards the stairs. They silently disappeared into the bedroom and moved the dresser to block the door, thus missing their youngest son muttering the words "Thanks, Dad."

••••

Framed by the moonlight, shafts of yellow penetrating the still night air, Dora sat on Dick's porch like a woman posed for a Hopper painting: sorrow and regret and homely defeat radiating from her in a heartbroken glow.

"Dora?" said Dick.

"She's gone," Dora said. "We lost her."

She handed Dick the note and he read it through gravely.

"This is my fault. I can't talk to her. I can't get her to talk to me. Couldn't. And I'm the one...who wanted to get divorced... and now she's gone. I'm sorry. I'm so sorry."

"Dora," Dick said as tenderly as possible. "She's not...you didn't..." The folds in his jowls extended angrily up and over his brow etching caverns in his forehead. "Let me tell you something: Fuck you. Did you think I would forgive you? Did you think you be absolved by sitting here and crying? It *is* your fault. Fuck you."

Dora sat stunned.

"And fuck this," he announced waving the note. "She's not gone. We're going to find her. Quit sniveling, get on your feet and come inside."

Instantly, Dick was on the phone with Jimbo's parents. They had received a similar note. His father was of the opinion that it was just a teenage thing and they'd be back soon—no need to get upset. Dick would have none of it, making a strident argument that he (Jimbo's father) was a fucking moron for thinking so. Dick further declared that they needed to notify the police with a description of Jimbo's car and that they needed to go through Jimbo's belongings for anything indicating where they might have gone. Jimbo's father again suggested he was overreacting. This bought a sincere but urgent inquiry as to whether Jimbo's father was fucking retarded. At this point Jimbo's mother got on the phone and indignantly informed Dick that if he wanted to do something useful he should go though his trashy slut of a daughter's things because she was obviously the one who drove Jimbo to this and just what kind of people let their daughter go out in t-shirts like that? Dick passed along his personal assessment that she was a cunt of substandard intellect, to which he added a curt "Fuck" of indeterminate meaning, and a warning that if they didn't try to find out where the kids were going he would contact the police and report that

Jimbo had kidnapped Jenna, then he would come over there and beat the living shit out of both of them on general principle. He concluded by yanking the phone out of the wall and whipping it across the room with a sharp, "Goddamit!"

Dick looked around in angry desperation. Dora had slumped to her knees in the middle of the living room, quivering silently.

"We'll get in the car. We'll go look ourselves," seethed Dick.

"Where?" asked Dora meekly.

Dick walked over to her and stared down at her.

"I'm sorry," she said again in barely a whisper.

Dick wanted to be a jerk. He wanted to ask her why she didn't call Ted. He wanted to scold her, and press her to turn her regret into appreciation of him. But he sank to his knees across from the woman he had once married and said, "It's not your fault. It's... We'll find her. Don't worry. We find her together. We're family."

Dora clutched his shoulders and fell against his chest. He returned the embrace. They kissed and kissed again, with the rapidity of lust-mad virgins, then fell to lovemaking with the limitless energy of youth.

••••

Attracted by the noises behind Otto's house, the officer carefully made his way to the back door, guided by the beam from his overtly phallic Maglite. Seeing the rear door window broken, he knocked again and made his call of "Police." He expected, and received, no answer. Reaching inside the broken window he opened the door for a look around. He eventually radioed for backup after following a certain lingering odor to the basement where he found a small but legally significant package of contraband, and enormous piles of potential contraband—including a few Tori Tornado dolls, one of which re-appeared a few days later as a gift for his niece.

••••

Throughout the neighborhood unblinking eyes looked on as Otto returned to find himself surrounded by what must have been a full two-thirds of the local police force. Children were put to bed from whence they immediately repositioned themselves to watch the proceedings from favored hiding places. In the surreptitious darkness of their upstairs bedrooms, their parents watched Otto hauled off in handcuffs. After brief exchanges of irresponsible speculation about the cause of such drama, the seedy flashing red lights and voyeuristic thrill compelled the men to lead their women to bed and their women to hope they were current on their birth control.

The next morning, cars caravanned off in an unfamiliar sequence, leaving most of the half-awake commuters disoriented.

EPILOGUE:
Legends of the Fall

Jenna was surprised to find her Mom in her Dad's house when Jimbo dropped her off less than a week later. She recited a tightly prepared and sincere preemptive speech about how she wasn't ashamed of running off, that she loved Jim and wanted to be with him, that no matter what one day they would be together, and as soon as they could they were going to try to get the hell out of this stupid town again.

Dora allowed the dust to settle from the speech and said, "Well, I guess you'll do whatever you want, won't you? Your father and I have decided to get back together. We'll be remarrying soon and taking a second honeymoon. It would be nice if you were around long enough to look after things while we are away. Sorry I can't stay and chat, honey, but I have to head over to the rec center. Your father should be home at the usual time. You'd better talk with him about how you're going to make up the time you missed at school. You don't want to flunk out in your senior year." She gave Jenna a warm hug on the way out, turning to say, "Oh and just so you aren't caught by surprise, your father has been dropping a lot of f-bombs lately. I'm hoping it's a phase."

Jenna found herself standing in a world not her own.

In fact, she and Jimbo had made it all the way to Seattle and found a motel where they didn't even ask for ID and only charged $25 per night. Over the next 48 hours Jenna became increasingly terrified of the place. She made Jimbo move the dresser across the door whenever they were in the room because of the threatening looks she got from the itinerant hooker population. For two days they had pounded the pavement looking for an inexpensive apartment in what Jenna called a non-crackhead neighborhood. Their fake IDs never failed but it seemed to them that every landlord had colluded to require first-and-last-month's-rent-plus-security-deposit, a phrase they uniformly slurred into a single word. Jenna went on fervent rants about profiteering landlords, oblivious to how much it made her sound like her hated father. Once, they stopped at an internet café to check for people seeking roommates. They found one that looked acceptable and a quick email exchange verified the price and revealed that they were also expected to pitch in with chores and "whatever", but when they drove to the place there was a semi-feral pit bull tied to the porch and a sinewy looking cretin in wife-beaters and a mullet on the porch. Jenna cried "Just drive away! Just drive away!" Each failure brought angry, non-specific complaints from Jenna. Jimbo began to feel beaten. He was supposed to take care of her, he was supposed to be responsible, and he grew more and more sullen and silent. Finding discarded hypodermic needles on the ground outside their motel window was the final straw. Both were secretly relieved to be going home.

Despite her declaration of eternal love, the trip had made Jenna realize that Jim may not be the one for her after all. She determined that she really needed someone who could take charge. Jim was sweet but he may just be a little too sweet.

Jimbo, in turn, was insufficiently judgmental to see Jenna as anything but a girlfriend to be loyal to. He was hurt when she dumped him a few weeks after their return, although he tried to stay on good terms throughout the rest of the school year.

It was years later, when Jimbo finally was out on his own and working full time while putting in night classes in engineering that he began to realize how deeply he resented her for her contemptuousness and incessant self-regard, even allowing himself to jokingly refer to her as his evil first girlfriend. Not that it mattered; he would never see her again.

For her part, it was about halfway through freshman year at Arizona State University when she had her final noticeable emotion for him: a tepid form of pity.

••••

Dora was extremely busy these days. Plans for construction were fairly set and she had moved on to administration. She had already appointed

Ted in Cement as something called "Building Consultant" and was actively lobbying Sarah to be something called "Programs Coordinator" and had declared Marlene Treasurer and Pammy Secretary, but Marlene politely demurred "considering her schedule and all," leaving Pammy to be Secretary-Treasurer. For these positions there would be no compensation, although once membership dues were collected she would likely be able to provide a stipend. For the most part, everyone was glad to help out when they could and generally pleased that weepy Dora seemed consigned to the past.

But when it came to running the Rec Center, Dora's primary management tool was passive-aggression, and friendships were reduced to duty. A year later when the center was up and running smoothly, she looked around at the first official meeting of the administrative board and saw none of her old friends. Ted in Cement had announced that he had no useful purpose to serve anymore, what with all the construction being complete, and so would probably "butt out" of any further proceedings. Pammy had cancelled out on so many meetings because "she had to deal with her boys," that Dora stopped asking. (While neither Pammy nor Marlene were available for duties, it was a sure bet they'd have their kids there every weekend, Dora observed bitterly.) Sarah at least collected some resumes for possible "program coordinators" before deciding she needed to "devote time to her yoga practice." Dora never understood why she couldn't do both. It wasn't like she had a family to think about.

In time she had broken Dick of his habit of profanity by pointing out to him that while there are people in the world who could effectively swear, he was not one of them. More broadly, Dick had changed, subtly. Though never less than constructive and helpful, he was occasionally distant and the deep-hearted affection they had felt the night that Jenna ran away had evaporated not long after their second honeymoon in Hilton Head. Strangely, though, he seemed to be making progress with Jenna. Dora would get nothing from Jenna during her weekly call home from Arizona; their communication was as empty as when she was a rebellious high school diva. In the end they always circled around to how Jenna was spending too much money. Then she would hand the phone over to Dick and from what she could tell they were actually talking, just having a casual, friendly conversation. Dick often broke out in laughter and looked at Dora with a grin.

Oh they were all happy with her as a doormat, a soppy sack of tears. But as soon as she was strong, as soon as she was confident, as soon as she no longer needed their sympathy, they lost interest. In private moments, when Dora allowed her bitterness full reign, her heart would race and her nostrils would flare and her eyes would grow dry and cold. She lost weight but the new lines in her face gave her the look of a crone.

••••

Of course, devoting more time to her yoga practice was not synonymous with running more classes. It was really more a matter of finding time to reconnect with herself so that she would have more acute awareness of the world, not just her yoga practice. Sarah had found herself adjusting her routines for Ted and her spiritual outlook had been subordinated to evenings watching TV with glasses of wine and exchanges of mundane details of the day. He never understood there was a problem.

When she kept bringing up her feelings he would always be sympathetic but he deflected everything, tried to make the situation sound perfectly acceptable. In time he took to brooding whenever she initiated these talks, then he'd get combative, then he'd check out.

Change was the way of things and not to be resisted. She had grown used to having Ted and Midge right next to each other in the front row for every class, and enjoyed her girlish chats with Midge about this and that—she had such a sweet naiveté about some things that Sarah felt guilty when she talked her into babysitting for Pammy and Flip—but habit in itself is contra-indicated, and so she decided to be grateful when Midge just stopped showing up one day (indirect contacts indicated that it was due to "school stuff") and they drifted apart. A few weeks later, Ted stopped coming: a further distancing.

There was meaning in the change that was being thrust upon her, and she dwelt upon it. She realized she should have trusted her first instinct regarding Ted in Cement. He was too conventional in his bland khakis and staid lifestyle. He was not right for her. She didn't regret her time with him for it served to confirm her judgment and she would have more faith in her own instincts in the future. That lesson, she determined, was change's reason.

Some weeks after their break up she felt a bit of sympathy for poor Ted. Over a small cup of Chunky Monkey, while looking out from Ben and Jerry's on a rainy evening, she had spotted him across the street talking with Midge. Clearly, he was not handling the break up well and had turned to Midge for any insights or inside information on what he might have done wrong. She thought of approaching them in an effort to mitigate his pain, but the urge passed. Theirs was a different path.

••••

The first time—and the last time—Midge babysat for Pammy and Flip was a bittersweet memory for Pammy. Flip had compromised on the motorcycle and instead bought a ten-year old Ford Mustang convertible (with Jimbo's help, of course). It was kitchen appliance white with a red interior, but he was going to have it painted black. In fact he was planning on all sorts of upgrades and customizations (with Jimbo's help, of course). The night they had Midge babysit for them, Pammy was delighted to be tucked away in a hidden, unlit, dead end side street, straddling Flip in the driver's seat with the convertible top down and her shirt pulled up over her breasts for all the world to see (although no one was actually looking). Sure, she knew that part of the reason for this was Flip's reaction to Midge in her clingy top and low slung jeans, but what the hell? It wasn't like she was above imagining it was Brad Pitt between her legs.

In time, the memory would come to be tinged with sadness when she realized it was the high water mark of her sexual existence. There was the time when they first met, when Flip was a jock in residence for the in-crowd and she was a flirty little cookie with the perkiest tits for miles around. There was no way they would ever have that quantity of sex again—nobody could—but the quality and intensity of their trysts during what she came to call the post-Otto period were reflective of a mature understanding of her libido.

But the kids were still a horror. And they still could never find a sitter. And Flip still never did anything without being scolded like a child. And let's face it; even at his best he wasn't totally reliable in the libido department. And once Jimbo started his new job all Flip did was go out to the Mustang and lift the hood like he was actually doing something on his own, probably so she wouldn't make him sell it. And his gut wasn't getting any smaller. Fighting the degradation of passion was hopeless.

Worse she had little outlet anymore. Sarah seemed to have drifted out of the neighborhood circle; Dora had become so standoffish when she saw her at the rec center that she tried not to make eye contact anymore—even on the days when the kids hadn't destroyed something or driven a lifeguard to want to drown himself. She could still talk to Marlene; they even playfully called each other "bitch" in an effort to keep the horrible emotions of their cul-de-sac battle royal suppressed. But Billy was around a lot more. The intimacy of Naked Tuesdays was gone. She bought a new dryer.

••••

Flip, Dick, and Billy were sharing a beer out on the

fountainless cul-de-sac island. Darkness came early now, and it would be months before any of them would leave the house without a coat. The blinding brightness of their subdivision had slowly despoiled from enamel-white and solar-yellow to a dire, dirty brown and a dreary, dull grey. The topic of today's conversation was the missing wheel cover on the right front of Billy's Honda Accord. There was gossipy speculation as to whether it had fallen off somewhere or it was stolen as a prank by "some kid," seeing as Flip noticed several neighborhood cars also missing the right front hubcap over the past couple of weeks. Dick reacted by glancing over at his Audi, recently purchased from Billy, and wondered why his hadn't been stolen, not realizing the expensive aluminum wheels had no hubcaps.

Dick was modifying every noun with a profane adjective, a practice that Flip and Billy no longer even noticed, but that he would have to be careful to curtail in other company. There were other things that had to be curtailed in other company. Like not driving his Audi to the Teacher's Union meetings, which is why he kept his trusty old domestic sedan. He was the new Local president and he had to play it like Richard III to stay on top. The extra income was another thing to keep from other company, since he was socking it away in a secret account just in case Dora decided to divorce him again. No way would he give up half his net worth next time.

Flip was talking about his new wraparound Oakley sunglasses. It seems they were the only things that make tolerable the weekend afternoons at the rec center pool with his monstrous offspring since they allowed him to ogle the "high school talent" unnoticed.

"Maybe if you had Playboy mud flaps for your Mustang they'd let you cruise with them to Dairy Queen," Billy suggested.

"I'll teach 'em how to tongue a tall cone."

"Fucking Flip. You are such a goddam filthy motherfucker. Shit. I teach some of those girls, you know."

"It's cool, Dick. I'll loan you the shades for gym class."

Typically as their conversation wore on it would turn to that crazy escapade of breaking into Otto's basement; how lucky they were, how stupid they were. It had been the talk of the neighborhood for weeks. Three police cars with flashing lights, hastily parked askew directly in front of Otto's house as everyone along the street peered through their living room bay windows at the spectacle of Otto being trotted off in handcuffs. He had a stupid grin on his face and seemed to be engaging the cop in friendly conversation as they loaded him into a back seat, carefully making sure he didn't hit his head.

The police blotter in the local paper revealed the next day that it was a "drug bust." Folks were stunned and there was much incredulous chatter about how a drug dealer could be operating in such a good neighborhood right under everybody's nose. Otto remained in the house for a couple of months but was never observed other than to see his car coming or going once every few days. There was speculation that he must be wearing a tracking device on his ankle.

When the neighborhood repopulated after the Thanksgiving holiday weekend, the house was empty and a For Sale sign was in front. When it was reported that Otto had successfully plea-bargained to possession rather than trafficking, with no jail time and a minimal fine (which he was able to pay on the spot with the cash in his pocket) the whole scandal rapidly dissolved from memory.

A loud crash came from Flip's house. Presently, Pammy stepped out onto the porch in a bathrobe and mud mask. "Flip! Would you get over here and help me please!"

They downed the dregs of their beers and headed for their respective homes.

••••

Missy had homework, which was absolutely ludicrous for a child her age, but she did seem to be doing better in her private school. Of course, that could just be the effect of the strange surroundings; the real test would come when she was no longer the new kid. For now, Billy assumed that homework was one way to show the parents that they were getting their money's worth. Since he now had a vested interest in Missy's education, he appreciated the gesture, however ludicrous.

"Done!" she announced. "Mommy, look at it!"

Marlene walked over and looked at the homework

with the gravity required to assure that Missy would derive satisfaction from her imminent praise. She was grateful for Billy's financial help and Missy's improvement was a great load off her mind. Billy didn't seem to fret about the money and mentioned that once he sold his condo it would be even less of a concern, but he never did seem to pull the trigger on that. He made noises about possibly renting it instead. But there it sat with his superfluous possessions quietly gathering dust on their way to vintage status.

She bobbed erratically in alternating waves of gratitude and uncertainty. Why wasn't he disposing of his condo? Why did he feel the need to join a different health club? Why didn't he want to be on the same wireless plan as her? Every time Marlene went through this examination, though, she realized the final question was, Why wouldn't he propose to her?

And then she felt silly. Did she really want another damn marriage on her resume? After all, things were going good. Billy was being attentive and loyal in the bedroom. He was a wonderful influence on Missy. He had given up his Audi. And if he hadn't opened his heart completely, he'd certainly opened his wallet. He'd even bought her a sterling silver lighter and crystal ashtray to hide in the garage. Maybe that was enough. Maybe it was as good as it gets.

And she would be happy until the next time he got home late with some bland explanation, then the waves would swamp her again.

"That's very good Missy. Why don't you put this on the counter by the door so we don't forget it in the morning."

Missy popped up and placed her homework by the door then hopped and spun over to where Billy was sitting and jumped into his lap.

Billy kissed her forehead and asked, "Missy, why don't you play with Tori Tornado anymore?"

"Too commercial," was the response. "Watch me dance ballet!" She began to twirl chaotically about the room.

There were times when Billy was awed by the difference in his life since moving to the suburbs. The odd thing was, he was still the same person below the surface. In his darker moments he thought that all life was a façade, a false construct for pain avoidance, and when the delusions he previously accepted began to fail, he simply found another role that masked the emptiness, as if he were an image rendered in Photoshop; various filters and settings produced differing effects and moods, but the underlying image—Outline Billy— was all there really was.

Whether the applied filter would one day include marrying Marlene depended on the day he asked himself. If it was a day without tension, a day when Missy was being adorable beyond belief, when he had barley awoken before finding himself tangled in idyllic intercourse, when Molly Maid had spent the previous day getting the place straightened and orderly, when they didn't fret over dinner and settled for Chinese take-out—those days Billy could easily see himself settled, finally, and he would silently vow to see a realtor and jeweler.

But then Sunday would come around and he remembered the low-burning exultation of easing in a chair for an afternoon of nothing at all, when friends would just drop by unannounced to share a beer and some inane small talk, just because everything was always so chilled out with him. And he thought about the times he would dress stylishly and bar hop on Thursday night, counting on encounters with friends and ex- and future lovers for entertainment—high comedy and low drama. And that Audi sure was a sweet car. And Otto's house had been purchased by a visiting academic from India who appeared to have brought along his entire extended family, including a trio of youngish females with those unfathomably dark sub-continental eyes and bustlines like nobody's business. Christ. Who was he to consider marriage?

Missy was all enthusiasm and joy and no timing whatsoever, causing her to fall over now and then, but she just kept turning pirouettes and calling on Billy and Marlene to watch.

"Look at that energy," Marlene said to Billy. "Youth is wasted on the young."

Billy agreed.